Sinners of Sanction County is one of the best story collections to come out of the American South in recent times. Writing in a spare, poetic style that fairly crackles with energy, Charles Dodd White makes his mark as a major new talent as he masterfully explores the raw beauty and pathos of life among tough people caught in bad situations. With this book, he has nailed the coonskin to the wall.

> — Donald Ray Pollock, author of *The Devil All The Time* and *Knockemstiff*

Bottom Dog Press

Sinners of Sanction County

≥ Stories ≥

Charles Dodd White

Appalachian Writing Series
Bottom Dog Press
Huron, Ohio

Bottom Dog Press, Inc.
P.O. Box 425 /Huron, Ohio 44839
http://smithdocs.net

Credits

Cover Photo: John Vacon, Farm Security Administration,
Library of Congress

Cover Design: Susanna Sharp-Schwacke

General Editor: Larry Smith

Acknowledgments

The following stories originally appeared in slightly different forms
in these publications:

"Age of Stone" in *Appalachian Heritage*; "Carrion" in *Necessary
Fiction*; "Controlled Burn" in *North Carolina Literary Review*;
"Hawkins's Boy" in *PANK*; "Confederates" in *Word Riot*; "Give
Up and Go Home, Jasper" in *Fried Chicken and Coffee*; "Killer"
in *Charlotte ViewPoint.*;"The Sweet Sorrowful" in *Necessary
Fiction;* "Winter by Heart" in *PANK,* and "A World of Daylight"
in *Fugue.*

The author would like to thank Rusty Barnes, Margaret Bauer,
George Brosi, Craig Buchner, Jackie Corley, Roxane Gay and
Steve Himmer for their editorial guidance. Also, to Robert Kloss,
for introducing me to the art of the remix. To Larry Smith, for
his ongoing support of these stories and his devotion to Appalachian
storytelling. For the friendship, whiskey, cigars and conversation,
I'd like to thank Robin Lippincott, Marilyn Lewis, Denton Loving,
Jake Pichnarcik, Mark Powell, Rosemary Rhodes Royston,
Brendan Van Voris and Crystal Wilkinson. And special thanks
to the North Carolina Arts Council for the generous fellowship
that has supported the completion of this book.

Table of Contents

For my bud, Page Seay

Hawkins's Boy

True, Hawkins buried his son more than once that summer. Wild dogs would get at the limbs glowing pale as quartz in the shallow ground, gnawing through the shroud of croaker sacks. They clacked their jaws, ceding nothing to sin or dignity. When he'd first buried the boy, Hawkins was too weak to break through the rocks and roots that choked the grave further down. Each time he had dug, the shovel tip sparked and split against the things already buried there—the iron so long corroded from sitting unused in the useless smoke house.

Hawkins would lie awake into that hour of the night and listen for the working of the dogs' teeth into tissue. The over and under shotgun lay slanted in the corner, the shape of a promise he would not place beyond his reach. But he did not take the gun and creep out of the house to shoot the dogs. If that had been his purpose, he would have crept, picked his naked soles over the tongue-in-groove. His deaf wife could not have heard him, but he knew the night had voices that could reach dead ears and pry open her sleeping mind like a hatch. So he would have crept had he ever stirred, had he ever drawn himself from behind the bars of pretended sleep. But he knew there were rituals to everything. He learned to prefer the stillness and listening to his boy's body disappearing into the dogs' rockslid bellies.

In the mornings he would rise and move out through the house with ease, clattering dishes in the kitchen while he boiled up a pan of old coffee. In the daylight he could take his time with this, unworried about waking his wife. She would not hear him now any more than in the night, but certain laws were suspended when the sun ripped itself up from the smoky ridge. Old laws, but frail as ash, and when these laws quit, even night monsters were permitted joy of the daylight. The paleness of the visible world freed him from thoughts that encrusted his skull like gems set tight against his brain, black as bibles.

That first morning he found hands and a hip joint. The fingers were grey at the tip but darkened to the color of a tattoo where the blood dammed. *The son's flesh mortified,* the churchers would have said. They would look for the hand of God in the decomposing boy, the rites that shored up their faith, and that was why he would always hate them. They did not understand. Neither they nor the One they worshiped did.

He collected and put the pieces of his son back in the ground. Then he went on back to the house and sat for the rest of the morning, watching the yard to see that the rest of the boy didn't come back up.

The mourners came later that afternoon to visit his wife. They could not use their hands to speak with her as Hawkins did, so they came and sat and scribbled their words out on the slate she kept, passing condolences like grammar school lessons, working diagrams for things that were supposed to give her peace. He sat in the kitchen and watched them. Because they were there to console, he wished them stricken. He knew that any wish he made, even a curse, was only breath spilled. But this still did not deprive him of his hate.

Once the mourners had sit with his wife for a while scratching with the chalk and saying pretty things she couldn't hear, they came at him, armed with pies, which wore tight hats of aluminum foil.

–And we'd only just heard that he passed.

–Yes, just this morning.

–You'll need to eat something. To stay strong.

–Reverend Coward told us. It was him that had us drive up to check to see if you needed anything.

–It's not much. Just a little blueberry. And a pecan.

–Hush. He doesn't need a recipe list. Poor thing.

–And he said he would be praying for you. The whole congregation would.

–Yes, every single one.

He remained as dumb as his wife, staring at them but committing no violence to the silence of the house. The women bunched themselves awkwardly together, hesitant and shuffling under his blank gaze until one of them made an excuse and then they were just gone.

He did not go to his wife, but remained sitting in the kitchen in that same chair he had the morning his boy dropped from his chair and strangled on his tongue. The boy had been perched there over a cup of Folger's telling of a fishing trip he had taken with a girl he was dating from Rabun Gap. The boy had been laughing and telling Hawkins how he (the boy) and this old girl had been laying out next to the lake with a pint of ABC store Wild Turkey between them and how she'd hauled out a whole pale tit from her powder blue bathing suit once she'd emptied the bottle. The boy had been so surprised at her willingness that he'd swung around to get his boots and jeans off, but he was further gone than he realized himself, and in his excitement to get a piece of some of that young stuff, he'd slung himself clear over the side of the clay bank and into the water. The boy and Hawkins were laughing so hard at this and Hawkins was so worried that his wife might somehow get wise to the wild goings on of what was being said that he didn't see the first sharp blow of the seizure strike the boy, his son's words caught in that fierce slash driving straight down from his brain into his body, setting his whole skeleton as rigid as a bolt.

And now the boy was dead two full days, the silence confirmed. When the boy had come into the world, he'd brought sound, shrieking with the cruel heart of a life ready to be lived. Hawkins remembered the night when the boy had shouldered his way out of his Mama, purple with outrage. How long now that awful night—forty-three years? My God, that long.

He remembered the labor come on his wife when she moaned with the sound of that deep sex love turned inside out. Terrible and hoarse but still somehow pitched like the quickened groans of coupling so that he was ashamed when he became a little excited at the sight of her pain. But then the panic had set in and there was no thought of pleasure when he realized the time to drive down off the mountain to the hospital in Sylva had passed, leaving them on their own. Only the surety of blood and the coming of his only son. Knowing the boy must be caught with his own mortal hands.

That second night after he buried the boy, Hawkins led his wife into the bedroom and sat with her while the wall-socket night light glowed over her tumbled shape like a little TV. He wished sleep on her before the dogs returned. He believed they would come, believed that they would slip out from the woods along with the fingers of evening fog. They had taken a set against him and there was nothing to do now but meet them.

When his wife finally settled into the deep breathing of unconsciousness, he went out to the porch carrying his shotgun and a full pack of Marlboros. He sat there all night smoking the cigarettes, watching and hearing nothing.

But once the ball of an early yellow sun appeared, Hawkins began to see the hunks of cadaver spread out before him like broken rinds in a harvest patch. The boy had arrived out of the dark without warning, carried in on the tide of night air and stranded in this brighter world. Again, Hawkins buried the boy, losing what little food he carried in his stomach from the smell of him.

A sheriff's deputy drove up under the hard noon sky. Gravel crunched and sprangled from under the big cleated tires of the Chevy. When it stopped, the deputy swung open his door and collected a notebook encased in metal with a plastic pen dangling by a silver beaded chain. His face wrinkled against the high sun.

He spoke Hawkins's name. The old man came up to talk with him.

–I knew some fool would get the law involved.

The deputy set the notebook on the Chevy's hood.

–Don't you recognize me, Mister Hawkins?

–Should I?

He removed his broadbrimmed hat.

–Your boy and me. We used to play ball in high school together. Down in Sylva.

Hawkins looked him over for a while and spat.

–Your family name is Painter, ain't it?

The deputy nodded, setting the hat back over his thinning brown hair, guarding what semblance of youth remained there.

–Yessir, my Daddy's Butch Painter. Second shift supervisor over at the paper mill.

Hawkins looked off at the road the deputy had driven up. The driveway cut into the sandbank, exposing a profusion of wild roots where trees on the hill above errantly sought purchase.

–I ain't paying no goddamn undertaker for what I went and done myself.

–Yessir. But there's still paperwork that needs filling out. Permissions for home burial. I brought em up here for you. To keep you from having to come into town to settle it.

Painter unlatched the steel box and pulled out a narrow sheaf of papers bound with an orange rubberband. Hawkins fanned the papers on the hood of the truck like a hand of hole cards.

–And that's all it's about. No other damn fool questions?

Painter toed his tire.

–Nosir. We all remembered the fits that would come on your boy. We've seen it ourselves over the years.

Even back there in high school on the ballfield it would happen.

Hawkins felt the old shame burn inside him, heating his face with clammy fever.

—There was nothing wrong with him, you know? He wasn't retarded or nothin. He was a smart boy. Always good about working. Never shirked a damned day in his life.

The deputy would not meet his eyes.

—Yessir. I always regretted not staying in better touch with him over the years. He was somebody you could always depend on. I remember that about him, sure enough.

Hawkins scratched his name on the forms where the deputy had put the little x marks and handed them back over. The deputy flipped through, ticking off each place to make sure the thing was properly met.

—Alright, Mister Hawkins. If there's anything else you folks need up here...

Hawkins went back to the house, not fit to hear another slight word.

That evening his wife woke him from a faint doze, working her hands in the air above his head, stitching words. Wednesday evening. The choir would be singing and she was intent that he drive her down to the church. Despite her deafness, she was always fierce about a choir. Hawkins knew there was no space for dis- agreement once her mind was set, so he got his hat from its nail. Together they went to the truck.

The drive was slow. A chilly fog had invaded the hills, blotting everything. The town's distant lights were a feeble guide, so Hawkins let the truck's headlights stab a safe distance through the riddled haze before tapping the accelerator. He reached for the radio dial but was stilled when his wife began to hum. She voiced an old tune, a hymn she preferred when the evening had come on and she thought he had stepped beyond earshot. But now she made the sound without regard for him. Her pale head rested against the pane of the passenger's window, the hollow base of her throat moving with the remembered vibrations that captured her idea of true song. A sound not without beauty, Hawkins realized. He tightened his hands to the steering wheel and drove down from the uppermost ridge to the town's steaming streets.

He let her off at the church's cement stoop, the golden rectangle of the open front door coffining her in electric light. They did not exchange antic gestures in their accustomed manner of physical speech. She knew he would leave her there and return at the appointed hour. This long fixed custom would not alter this night, their grief disturb nothing.

Once she had gone inside, he drove the empty streets for some time, circling the single downtown block. He counted each lap when he sighted the false clock. Down through the years, the sight never failed to anger him. The electric yellow digits above the Central Bank sign read 8:23 AM. Some fool had switched the evening and morning registers more than a decade ago and the clock was forever telling the exact time at the opposite end of each day. The error was enough in the way of poor number management to lead Hawkins to withdraw every account he had sitting in the bank and place the last dollar in a fire proof safe he kept under the bedroom floor. He had told his boy that he'd rather be a fool with buried money than a man who would trust someone without a proper notion of night or day.

As he circled round once more, however, the idea of that hour put Hawkins in the mood for a hot breakfast. He had not eaten since the work of the morning had claimed what food he'd been able to keep down, and now his guts were a wronged and pained enemy. He saw that the Downtown Cafe was open. He turned in and cut the engine.

Inside, cigarette smoke striated the air. When he passed through, the visible waves circulated briefly before closing back over him like oil.

Hawkins took a seat at the counter and studied the whiteboard for specials, but when the night waitress came and asked for his order, he said to bring him only black coffee and eggs.

–Don't want any meat or nothing?

He stared into her pretty and catatonic face. She shook her head and went away when he said nothing.

A television hung from a suicidal angle above a poster of a stock car driver. A beer commercial was playing. Two men at the far end of the counter wearing Stihl and John Deere caps were paying scant attention to the pictures which played across the milky screen while they talked and smoked. Hawkins knew neither of them, so he didn't attempt a word.

While he waited for his meal, he thumbed through a newspaper splayed on the Formica. He did not read so much as skim his eyes over the type, looking at the pictures of the high school baseball team and a girl who'd been reported kidnapped. When he grew tired of this, he pushed the paper away and looked down at his hands on the counter. Large and rough, but now also grown weak with age. What things he'd done with these hands.

His food came and he ate silently. Years of this odd habitual quiet lay on him. The more he remained still and without words, the more notice he drew from other people. He could feel the black stares of the men beneath the TV, their judgment. The waitress too, when she came with her little paper tab with doodled smile. He couldn't bear their hate. He paid and left.

The streets were tattered with fog, as if the sorrow inside him was spun through the nighttime world, mean and deprived. He went to the truck and took the .38 snub nose from under the driver's seat and locked everything, leaving the truck in the cafe parking lot while he walked the streets alone.

He kept his hands in his pockets, hiding them. They were ugly weights pinned to the rest of him, the bones in his wrists like loosened brads, fingers left flapping. When he was young, his hands had served well as trustworthy tools, but when his wife lost her hearing, Hawkins found the strong claws he'd once carried with pride were ill suited for threading words. His squared fingertips were slow and dead when it came to fine work. Without easy language, his wife had receded from him over time. Through no fault of her own, Hawkins realized, but because of *these hands*. Because he could not talk with her well, the words they exchanged became merely functional. And Hawkins had come to learn that function was not a place where love could survive long.

As he walked on he saw that so much of the town was utterly dark. Only the green pools of security lights on the grass out at the recreation fields. He quickened towards them, drawn on by the memories there. His boy cutting across the right field to snatch a hard shot down the foul line. The pop of the ball skipping to his mitt and the masculine groan as he flung it home.

Inside the field gates, Hawkins became a younger man. He was a father again and there were the sounds of people talking around him. He eased himself onto the aluminum bleacher, the seat crying softly; this meant nothing to him amid the babble of all that remembered noise. So prevalent and easeful. So unmourned. The night's steady engine hummed, and he grew attentive. No longer the fear of others, just this patch of quiet world and time spreading inside him like music. What way was there to capture this sound alone?

The pistol in his hand rose. The muzzle level with his ear, trained skyward.

The first shot brought pain. But the others, fired off rapidly by each ear, lopped the sensation clean away, like a discarded limb into an amputee bucket. He felt the warm, leaky silence take him as he dropped the pistol and started out towards all that aching dark.

Controlled Burn

Sheriff Gene Wilcox had the decency to drive up to the ridgeline where we were breaking ground on the new development to tell me himself of the government's coming crime. I'll hand him that. There are other men who would have sent a deputy. More generous man than me might call that kindly. But I've never been a friend to those that pin a badge over their hearts.

He pulled his unmarked Crown Vic up to the tail end of the zigzagged ruts where the bulldozer sat idle and he cut his engine. It was lunchbreak and my Mexican boys were off under a shade tree eating their tortillas and menudo. My feet were propped on my old Igloo cooler, tall boys of Old Milwaukee and Pabst sweating inside. It was getting on to that time of the afternoon when cracking one open would be a shame worth bearing.

He hauled himself out of his cruiser and threw his hand up, and I told him to come on and grab him a seat. His guts ballooned when he eased his carcass down on the chair, the aluminum legs groaning and digging little wellshafts in the sand.

"You ain't gonna care for this, Dayton," were the first wicked words out of his mouth.

"Wanna sip of something?" I ignored him, toeing the cooler.

"You got Co-Cola?"

He read the look on my face like he'd chalked it there himself.

"I guess I'd better not then."

He sat there passing a pen knife over the white rims of his fingernails, shaving air, killing time.

"Well?" I asked. "I know you ain't up here to ask how high my corn patch is standing."

He tore a shred of hangnail and spilled some of the breath he'd been catching.

"It's your daddy's place, Dayton. The tract up there above Parson's Den. They've found something."

"They?"

He spat dryly.

"FBI. Called me up there to have a look just this morning."

I popped the cooler open and dragged my hand through the ice for the first can I came across. I could feel my fingers turning baby pink from the cold.

"You're about two months too late for April Fools, Gene."

"I wish that was the case. I surely do. But this is serious."

I looked over his shoulder at a pair of turkey vultures turning in the haze, their clockwise circling seeming to screw down a big lid of hot air over all the greenly slumping mountains. There was some kind of old-fashioned peace in it.

"Some bastard had him a weapons cache up there," he went on. "One of these end of the world nuts. A post man or some such. Booby-trapped the whole thing with dynamite and tripwires. Hell, with as much as he's supposed have stuck up there, it's enough to blow the top of the mountain off. Government wants to burn it out. Do a controlled burn. Dig firebreaks between the ridgelines. That way they can keep from hauling it all down and risk having it blow up on 'em."

I took a drink of the Pabst. It passed down my throat like a sad song going back the way it had come.

"What about my daddy's old hunting cabin?"

He studied the silent black tongues of his shoes.

"It's on the wrong side of the creek, Day. There ain't no way to save it."

"Well," I said. "I guess I won't be taking your word on that."

After he'd left, and once I put my mind around what Gene had said a good long while, I had the Mexican boys knock off early and pile into the truck. Most of them rode in the back along with the rattling gear. My head man Ernesto sat up in the cab with me, smoking a Benson and Hedges.

Most of the Mexicans got off at the crossroads, but I drove Ernesto up to his place, the illegal trailer park out behind the back of the elementary school in Cullowhee. His family lived in a beaten box that looked like something that had fallen out of the sky and been kicked across the yard by a mean kid. Wasps jerked back and forth through broken windows and stove-in walls. A brown woman stood over a pair of babies in diapers and matching yellow tee shirts. If she had have been twenty pounds lighter, she might have been something to look at.

"I guess you wouldn't be interested in making some extra dollars this weekend?" I asked.

He stared out the windshield at all that heat, the yard grown up with tall blond weeds, seeing something other than that pitiful excuse for a homeplace for him and his family. Few men I've known can look on the sorry truth of something and admit it's as bad as it is, even if the admitting is to themselves alone.

"You want help with your father's cabin," he said, breathing out lung smoke.

"That's right."

He shook his head, not looking me in the eye.

"That cabin's going to burn, Mister Dayton. Didn't you hear what the sheriff said? Too dangerous. You should never think the law will allow you to do such things."

He pitched his cigarette butt out the window and swung the door open.

"Be careful, Mister Dayton," he said, walking on up to his trailer, putting his flat hand in the air to say goodbye.

I stared up as his little rotten trailer on the hill for a while, then drove the truck back out on the rutted drive and headed to the hardtop. I sat there and smoked a cigarette before I decided to ride up to Lookout Cove, going on to what everybody now called Tommy's Place.

When I cut the truck's engine, there was nothing but a mountain of quiet in that yard. It seemed to be empty at the big house. I sat there and remembered how the place had taken shape under my hand more than thirty years ago. Remembered too the year Martha, the boys and me had wintered in a kerosene heated lean-to while I dragged the house's timbers into their proper angles, pulling something like a home up out of the ground.

It was nearly five years since Martha had died, leaving the place so lonesome and gutted out, nothing but the ghosts of our now grown children running around on those moaning floorboards. I'd been happy to sell it to Tommy and move down country a ways. My trailer and cats were about all I could take at the time, and besides, Tommy seemed all set on starting a family, fathering his own passel of boys. But, of course, all of that has come to nothing.

When I got out I could hear the garden hose spray around on the side. I knew that would be my son's wife, Maybelline, tending her tomato and okra patch. She is one hell of a good looking woman, blond headed and deep through the curves. She wore cutoffs and a tanktop sucked tight to her chest. In her hair she had a blue bandanna wrapped up snug. If I had of been Tommy, I would of put a softer shape around her middle years ago.

I said hello and flirted with her a bit. She smiled and told me Tommy was around back. I went around and found my son on the screened-in back porch, the door propped open, letting every description of mosquito into the place. He leaned over a vise locked down on an upright fishhook, tying flies. I'd never once lifted my hand to cast a flyrod. Never saw the fish in any of these mountain waters that a spinner reel and a piece of corn wouldn't catch just as good as any such fancy rig. But Tommy'd picked up the hobby from some of those Asheville hippies he'd been known to run with. Hell of a man for expensive habits that have nothing to do with the way he was raised.

"What brings you up, Daddy?" he asked, not looking up from his magnifying glass and blunt scissors.

"Just driving through is all."

"That right?"

"It is."

"You wouldn't mind a drink of something, I bet."

I allowed that I wasn't allergic. He tipped back in his chair and opened the mint green door on a fridge the size of a TV. He tugged out a couple of Budweiser longnecks, popped the caps and handed one to me.

"It'll beat a summer day," I said, grateful for the chance it gave me to think. It was a while before I got around to what I'd come up for. "Actually, son, there is something."

"Course there is."

"You don't have to say it like that."

"How you want it said, then?"

"Like nothing, Tommy."

We drank and watched the mosquitoes drift in and light on the backs of our hands, flexing their slim checkered legs before we'd take a swipe and they'd swirl off, just to do it again in another couple of seconds.

"I need your help, is all. There's a controlled burn being laid down up on Parson's Den. If we don't do something, your Grandaddy's cabin won't make it."

He smiled down at the tops of his sandals and pinched the bill of his Duke cap between his fingers.

"I thought that old place ruined years ago. It's got to be eat up with termites."

"It ain't that bad."

"Bad enough, I guess."

I knocked back the rest of the Bud.

"Well, I ain't asking for your charity."

I started to leave.

"Don't go running off," he said, standing up. "When you need me, Daddy?"

I very nearly told him to go to hell. Very nearly.

"First thing Saturday morning," I said. "Make sure you've got your chainsaw and some bar oil."

He snapped the bottleneck up from between his veed fingers and sucked on the glass.

"Bring some coffee, will you?" he said.

I was up before the chickens. It's been that way since Martha passed on. Never can sleep through the early hours of the morning. Too much haste in a man's life when he has as little time left as I do.

I went on to the kitchen and put a can of Kozy Kitten on the electric can opener. As soon as it started turning, I had cats dripping off every chair and table in sight. I plopped the pale mealy mess out onto half a dozen pie plates and let the brats set to it, their purring so loud I could hear it above the Mr. Coffee.

"Eat up, fatbodies," I told them. They meowed back.

It was just light when I pulled up to Tommy's place. He was already out on the front stoop, his gear piled up in a little tower. I left the truck running while I got out and helped him stash everything in the bed. I smoked a cigarette while he sipped from my thermos and then we went on.

I took the 107 up past one of the gated communities near Cashiers. I'd helped build all those places up there nearly a decade back. Once we were down on the opposite side of the creek with the road flung out, we could see up to the distant ridges, each of those big houses stuck to the side of the mountain like flying saucers that had crashed there and been left stranded. The big glass A frames shone like grit in sand.

"A damn shame," Tommy said, his mouth loose above the black plastic rim of the thermos.

I glanced back at the development.

"What's that supposed to mean?"

"Just me talking. It doesn't mean anything."

"The shit it don't."

"Watch your blood pressure, Daddy."

We drove for a piece.

"I guess you're forgetting all them houses up there is what paid for your college. Paid for that house you're living in, too. Your Momma sure as hell never had a problem with it."

"No, Daddy. I'm not forgetting any of that."

We pulled off at a station a ways up to top off the gas. From there on all the way up to my daddy's place, we didn't trade a word.

I took us into the property through the back way. The main route was blocked off by the government to keep campers and hikers out of their planned hell. The dirt drive was carved deep from the weather and the years. It was tight with overgrowth, branches and vines slapping the windshield and the top of the cab. Caught limbs scratched up from beneath the truck's floorboard. I could feel it through my boots, a dull uneasiness on the soles of my feet.

"You remember turkey hunting up here?"

For a long time I didn't think he was going to answer me.

"Yeah, I remember it," he said. "Seems like another life."

"It does, well enough."

Once we got up to the cabin I pulled off on a hard gravel bank on the high side of the property. It was cool under the shade trees and not too buggy. A little creek that never carried a name floated by. It never had been anything to anyone, and still wasn't much more than a dimple through sand flats. From where I was standing, I could see clear to the smooth bottom. It was only a matter of a few inches from the surface to the bed. But still I could remember how it had been there for all of the fifty-two years I'd been coming up, running a course as regular as a racetrack, always scant and shallow, never digging a place for itself in the sediment. I wondered how that could be. How a stream could bleed itself down through the years without making some scar on the earth.

I went on to check the hunting cabin while Tommy brought all the gear down front. It had been near two years since I'd stepped foot in the old place. The door had come loose at the top hinge so that the board was jammed until I lifted with all I had and swung in. Inside it was dank as a grave. Spider webs hung from the roofbeams, going silver and trembling in the sudden gush of sunlight. I put my hands out in front of me, running the webs through with the ends of my fingers. The webs clung. I went back out and clapped and dusted my hands until I got the whole cloudy mess off. Tommy didn't offer to lift a finger.

Once our gear was settled, I showed him what I intended. We needed to cut away as much highstanding timber as we could, reduce any fuel the wildfire might find as it came close to the cabin. Tommy brought his chainsaw out and we started felling every tall tree around the place, laying the fat and skinny trunks alike with great booms against the ground. I'd spell him occasionally, though there wasn't much hard work in what we were doing. Not with the big orange Stihl notching angles on the trunks and gravity doing the rest. It was something else to see those trees chewed up like that, vines ripping from the top branches on the way down like wigs being snatched off the heads of dying women. By early afternoon we'd cut a good perimeter fifty feet deep in every direction. We sat down on the cabin's porch and ate what we brought with us, looking on the country we had just opened up.

"You think that's far enough to keep the fire off?"

"We can only pray," I told him.

That night we sat up on the porch and watched heat lighting shake itself loose somewhere far out in the dark, hoping it would turn into rain, but it never did. Under that sad sky I remembered the nights I'd sat out there on that very spot as a boy and listened to rain snapping on the tin roof like gunshots. Could still see the way my daddy and his hunting buddies would holler and carry on, telling lies and helping each other to their bunks when they'd gone and got stumbling drunk. It was scribbled down deep in my brain to become the kind of man my father was. But something had happened in those years in between. Looking at Tommy I could see it, as plain as plyboard: a space between the two of us had grown up that no matter of talking or sitting would ever change.

I don't remember making my way to my bunk and falling asleep. Only the grey light throbbing at the edges of my eyes the next morning and Tommy standing over me, a pair of coffee mugs in his hands.

"They've set it," he said

I swung my feet down and shook out my boots in case a scorpion had nested in them overnight. I could smell the smoke, sharp as daylight.

We walked on out to the yard and looked down the mountain. We couldn't hear anything yet, only see the smoke coming on through the trees like true evil given shape.

"Hell of a thing to do on a Sunday," I said.

He gave me one of the coffees. It was pure heat in my hands. We stood there until the sun was full up, the smoke moving on its own sick yellowed tide, the backlight of daytime making the trees seem to smolder before the fire had even reached them, an illusion out there amongst things I thought I knew. Once I'd bottomed the mug, we could hear flames faintly cracking.

The fire, the bigness of it was a monster coming to this world like true hate. Birds flew past, carrying the smell of scorch. I moved out there with Tommy among the felled timber of our fire break, waiting for the great wrecking to come, the entire measure of whatever unnatural force those men had put in motion. The sky was blue that morning, blue and endless. But when the smoke came, the color drew back. There was only the smoke, and me and Tommy standing in the middle of it, knowing the land was giving up on all of us.

The explosions came from far down the hill, a good half a mile off. Even so, the first detonation sounded like the earth's spine had been jerked up and snapped clean in two. Then, nearly a minute later, the secondary explosions went off in a regular chain, dull and sharp alike, the stockpiled bullets and dynamite cooking off, shaking the ground beneath my feet. It was enough to make Tommy sling his coffee out on the dirt and begin loading gear in the truck. After another few minutes of watching the smoke come on, I started helping him.

It's hard to say when I saw the first of the fireline. The smoke was a strange mirror, bending everything around so that what I saw may have been with my eyes or my head. But when I could feel the coming heat on my face like a sunset, I knew we had to leave.

Tommy was already sitting in the truck with the engine running when I headed up. I got in and he pulled off without a word. We kept the windows rolled up and the air conditioning off to keep from pulling the fumes inside. All around the road, the land seemed to be closing down around us, the trees leaning in like a tunnel of old bones.

I talked him up to a wrecked ridgeback the old sawmillers used to call Tickle Cut. It was high and clear of the burn area. I had him pull over.

"Why stop, Daddy? There ain't nothing to see."

Even as he asked it, he slowed and eased up onto a solid bank. He cut the engine and we both got out.

We could see the whole drunken spread of fire coming on through the valley, a bright thread of flames and the bundle of smoke like long grey hair in the wind. It was eating everything up, coming on to the cove where Daddy's cabin sat. We were too far away to hear anything, but Godamighty it was burning now, tearing the mountains apart. The hell that men had put there was running a true course, and there was nothing in the world to stop it. I stared at the burn, wondering how a man could put a spark on all that, how we had let it happen. I don't know exactly why I kept watching, why I didn't let Tommy take me on home. But I wanted to drive the pain of it through my eyes and into my brain. Bury it there like a hot needle.

Carrion

There were no secrets good or bad between Daddy and me, but once he got popped for that third DUI coming out of Highlands, he brought me into the family business of carcass shopping down around Seneca and Greer. That's where he showed me the bloody back rooms of old trailers and sheds, the wrecked deer corpses dangling from their hind ends, forelegs hanging down towards the floor like they meant to gain solid ground with just one more stride.

His was the simple business of scooping up of carstruck bucks and does before the state police phoned in a roadkill site to the county removal detail. Made for decent enough money in the right circles, especially given what Daddy liked to call "these peculiar economic times." He said to me that there was no shame in the use of slaughter that would otherwise spoil and prove nothing but a hazard to commuters who cared not a whit whether it was the government or us who hauled the dead out of sight, freighted them down to the men with meat saws who would turn around and sell the cuts for pretty much pure profit once they'd paid us for our troubles and risks that involved dodging eighty mile per hour traffic in day or night, snow or sun.

What I didn't know, of course, was just how much Daddy was skimming off the top before he handed over my share, the paper bills gore smudged at the tips like the lipstick kiss around the rim of a lady's beer glass or her cigarette butt. I was only seventeen, he said, only seventeen and liable to run him clear off the road. But still he figured it was better in his mind to hazard steel mangling up around his body than to risk highway troopers catching him out with a suspended license, which everybody knew would get him sent upstate for a good six months of lockup if not more. So he'd show me bits and pieces of what to look for on a salvaging trip. That's what he called our highway drives, "salvages," a word that's always sounded mean on the tongue to me, like some issue of a match and kerosene.

He would put me behind the wheel while he leaned up from the backseat where he could take his drinks at ease and talked in my ear, his breath a snaking mad spice around my head. We would head down in that old restored Pontiac that coughed and spit exhaust smoke, and he would show me how to spot a hard median, kicking gravel all across the macadam when we pulled a quick stop. In time I got damn good, sometimes covering a couple of hundred miles of interstate to find a decent kill or two, trussing them up in the trunk, or sometimes, if they were too big, lashing them to the hood, the smell of their blood carrying straight through the vents, coppering up the air.

There were times we would have to stop, have to skim off the main run and drive up the access roads, blundering down old state routes, sometimes mile after mile, hunting up a liquor store or some truck stop honky tonk that would sell brown paper booze under the table. Time would just seem to peel open for him, and he'd forget the hours still ahead while he sought the bottom plumb line on any bottle of brown liquor in his fist.

Our last time out salvaging, Daddy shunted us up a good hour off the track. He'd torn through a pint of George Dickel and his breath was a hot ache on the back of my neck. He was talking about all the times he'd taken me hunting as a kid and then he remembered how once I'd dumped out his secret flask on the dirt when he wasn't looking. He'd promised my Mama he wasn't going to drink anymore, and I had poured out the whiskey, afraid of the times he'd drink and pull his Ruger revolver on me when I stepped back into the deer camp from going to pee. He would have gotten so blind drunk that he couldn't recognize the face of his only son when I stepped back under the hard circle of lantern light.

He was in my ear talking, and I wanted to put the pictures inside my head to rest, so I dropped my foot down a degree or two on the accelerator, letting the road surround us with its hum. He didn't seem to notice, so caught up with whatever it was he thought he was trying to prove to me. I let the country just flow past. The land beyond the road was raw, not snowing or raining but looking like it might, black winds blowing out of black foothills and the sky scratched with something ancient and flat. For hours, in all that stretch we saw only cars and trucks huffing out their smoke. It was at that switching hour between day and night, the time where light falls down in on itself like it's finally given in to gravity when he saw the buck.

The deer lay in the center lane, untouched somehow even though the cars were just inches on either side of it when they whipped past. I swerved off over the rumble strips, the whole car shuddering until I got clear to the emergency lane. Daddy was out of the car before I could throw the transmission into park, stumbling into the headlight bored twilight. Cars zipped on by, honking as he wobbled across the lanes, fighting his way towards the corpse.

It was a big old buck that would have gone a good two-fifty on the hoof if it went an ounce, laid out with antlers above his head like an unfinished halo of bone. Daddy turned his head to me and smiled so wide I thought his chin would drop. Just then, another heavy vehicle came flying, a heavy cement truck, and Daddy realized it meant to cut his find in two. His hand loosed its stranglehold on the empty bottleneck and the glass cracked forgotten on the hardtop. I yelled for him to come back, but he didn't hear, didn't hear as he reeled out towards the middle of the road, waving his hands over his head like a lost man would for a search party, the thin comets of oncoming headlights showering him. I yelled again, but he was there now, jumping up in the air, kicking his feet like they were hurt by any contact with the ground. I wanted to turn away, to not see then spray of blood that would be my last memory of him, but the truck came so fast there wasn't time to close my eyes.

The tires laid out a long scream as the truck jerked towards the left, a blind lane switch that crushed only air. The loud horn came back, bellowing like a huge wronged beast, but kept driving on down the road into the gathering night. Daddy looked back at me, laughing and shaking like someone had him on strings. He turned back towards the buck and grabbed hold of the antler tine, raising his trophy's head.

But then something happened. As soon as Daddy touched hand to horn, the resting life of that deer shot up through its muscle and bone, a current that shook it from a sleep men would never know. Daddy staggered back like he'd been struck, the buck coming to its uncertain legs like it had just been foaled, tossing its flattened black snout. It came straight at Daddy, slow but steady, shivering its head and grunting, drunk from temporary resurrection. Daddy stumbled back to the edge of the road and screamed for me to follow him to the car. When I got in, he was already in the back seat breathing hard, his head rolled back on the seat rest, his face pale as a truce flag.

Killer

Even though Hiram was a boy, his father Sloane saddled both mules in the dark and cold and together they rode out of the valley toward the rising sun, neither of them talking, silent as any other pair of men. Before daybreak they were alone, two figures leaning into the long climb, but when the sun flushed the mountains pink, the birds flew off the roost in search of prey, winging crosswise in search of nocturnals who had overstayed their welcome. The crows were always first above the ridgelines, single scouts against the sky, noisome and wary when they spotted the riders. Later came the buzzards, rising silently as they caught morning thermals, gliding without perceptible motion. Circling and waiting for whatever fatal gift might fall.

After they had breached the gap, Sloane and his son stopped and shared biscuits wrapped in grey handkerchiefs, watching the birds and sipping from a jug of lukewarm coffee. They talked of the hunt ahead, the boy's first chance to kill and become a man, just as generations of his male kin had passed into manhood further back than the father could ever trace.

The boy's mule shifted under him.

"She ain't sitting easy, is she?" Sloane asked.

"She'll do, I figure."

When they moved on, the country opened up. They kept to the ridge, not wanting to hazard the tangled laurel at the lower elevation. Sloane knew the hunting party would be in camp by noon, so he pressed hard to make as much progress as the land allowed. Pulling one of his little cigars from a leather pouch, he crimped it in his mouth. The boy watched.

"You ain't old enough," Sloane said.

"I didn't say nothing."

"I'm just saying."

They didn't stop for water until it was midday and had come out from some of the high country and found a well at the end of a box canyon red with clay. Afterwards, they rode out, keeping the trace until a hungry suppertime when they took the route west, the distant clouds trailing vapor like beads of blood. The mountains ranged before them, tin cut jagged and nailed to the sky. Sloane checked his pocket watch against the decline of the sun.

They rode, their heads and shoulders bent before the weight of their arrival. Then the darkness came on them, flooding the world with a deep blindness.

When Hiram heard the dogs baying down in a valley of oak and fir, night was full and the timber had taken on weird tongues, but there was no mistaking the sounds of encampment. Against the trees, firelight pulsed and shivered. The hunting party appeared alternately in silhouette and licks of color, chased into creation one moment as men and the next as ghosts.

"Why Hell, if it ain't the Tobit men!" a man with a beard as orange as rust shouted. He strode across the camp, wrung Sloane's hand and clapped him on the shoulder. The men sitting and squatting around the fire with small mess tins of beans turned shadowed faces. Hiram stood holding both mules, looking with awe on a site as pagan as Baal.

"We'd 'bout given up on you for tonight," said the bearded man. "Figured this boy's momma had clapped a stopper on your plans."

Sloane looked at his boots. "Nosir, I told her churchgoing didn't have nothing to do with deer hunting."

Hiram did not look at his father. Sloane fused his eyes to the ground.

In half an hour it was time for the men to retire to two big canvas tents, accommodations that were no more than large tarpaulins draped from a taut rope between two trees and staked down along the side. Both ends were open to the evening air so that the men had to mummify themselves in wool blankets to keep warm. They made pallets of straw and dried moss, and within minutes they were snoring gape-mouthed, oblivious to the canvas roof popping in the wind.

When Sloane shook Hiram awake, the boy knew pain complete. Not from his father's touch, but because his body ached from the previous day's travel. It was hard for him to suppress a sob as he raised himself on one elbow.

"What's wrong?" Sloane said.

"Ain't nothing. Just sleepy is all."

"Here's some coffee," Sloane said, pressing a warm tin cup into the boy's hands. The hands, once hard, were now as soft as a girl's. Hiram nodded and drank, trying to find a way to sit so that he didn't wince. Sloane watched him.

"You remember you was the one who said you wanted to come along?"

"I ain't said nothing, Daddy."

"Get ready then. They already got the dogs up."

When Hiram walked out into the campsite, his single barrel .410 broached and hanging from his arm like a fractured limb, he saw a young man with fine blond hair, caught occasionally in a draught of the morning fire's smoke. He squatted before a tub of soapy, steaming water, scrubbing at a submerged pile of metal plates and eating utensils. His hands and forearms were red from the water.

"Your turn tomorrow," the youth said, smiling as he bent back to his chore.

Hiram walked to the edge of the treeline and saw the first paling of the morning to come. The songbirds were making a racket up in the hills, their melody joining the descant of the soughing trees, each separate tone made liquid as the sound moved through the dying and already dead leaves. The other men talked and smoked, readying themselves to test their legs and hearts against the mountains that held their quarry.

"You ever been on a deer drive before?" the boy with the cookware asked.

"Nosir, I have not."

The boy laughed. "I ain't no sir. I ain't but fifteen. Name's Henry."

He extended a slippery hand. Hiram took it and tried to wipe his own hand dry without the other boy seeing.

"How old are you?"

"I'm eleven next month," Hiram said, drawing himself up.

Henry pinched his chin between his index finger and thumb, stroking imaginary whiskers.

"Eleven, huh? Why I guess that was about the time I shot my first buck. Maybe that's a omen."

Hiram didn't know what he should say.

"That's a pretty gun you got there."

"It's borrowed. It belonged to my brother."

"Belonged?"

Hiram sawed his hand's bony edge against the bridge of his nose.

"He ain't living."

"I'm sorry to hear that and all," Henry said. "But a borried gun is good luck, don't you know? As long as it ain't bloodied. Shooting another man's gun that's already kilt something means the meat won't be no good. It ain't bloodied is it?"

Hiram looked down at the shotgun and shrugged.

"Naw, probably not," Henry decided. "Except maybe for rabbits and squirrels and such and that don't count when it comes to deer."

Henry tipped the basin and held his hands over the softly clattering plates to keep them in place as he dumped the dirty water on the ground.

"Let me show you something else, shore enough," Henry said. Together they went to the back of the tent and unfolded a hide case. He stood, holding the rifle across his body. Dropping it barrel down with one hand, he reached into his jacket's breast pocket and drew out three brass cartridges, pressing them into the spring loaded receiver with as much care as he would nursing a newborn.

"She's something, ain't she," Henry said with wonder. "I worked all last summer to save up for her. This is a Winchester. The gun that won the West." He bent on one knee and trained the muzzle at the peak of the tent as he smoothly opened the lever far enough that Hiram could look into the chamber where the round was seated. "After I shoot, I throw the lever all way forward and it kicks out the shot bullet and puts in the next one. It's better see, cause I can get a second shot off real quick if I need to without taking my finger too far off the trigger."

"That's something else," Hiram said.

"Shore. It's one of those modern miracles, I guess. Hey, we better get going or they're fit to leave us."

When the two boys stepped outside, the armed men had already begun to draw away from camp in single file, a dozen or so, moving quiet and solemn. Only the dog handlers remained behind, chewing tobacco and talking over the anxious dogs. His father, far ahead in the party, had made no effort to wait for him. Instead of trying to catch up, Hiram trailed along at the end with Henry.

They reached the ridgeline in less than half an hour, peeling off from the column in hundred yard intervals so that the men covered the full gap at the head of the valley. Henry and Hiram were the last to take up their positions. Henry made sure Hiram was settled into place in a shallow depression between a pair of poplar trees, blurring his silhouette against a clutch of sawvine with thorns finer but sharper than barbed wire.

"That should do it there. Just remember to listen for them dogs. I'm gonna drop off this next little holler over yonder if you need anything."

Hiram watched Henry's back fade into the pale grey woodland and leaned forward in his natural embrasure, trying to duck as much of the savage wind as he could. His broadbrimmed hat did nothing against the cold. His ears ached and the nape of his neck felt like someone had poured a pitcher of creek water over it.

The dogs were late in coming. The wind had backed shortly after the line of waiting hunters settled in, carrying the men's scent in the direction of the valley where the dogs were supposed to drive, forcing the delay. After a while, the wind began to die as the sun rose to the treetops. Hiram struggled to keep his eyes open in a patch of sunlight. He drew his knees up against his chest and leaned the shotgun against a rotting log, letting his mind wander.

Time sank and the world grew immense. Hiram felt himself drawn across it, like a hide stretched veil-thin across a drying rack. He may have dreamed, but the sounds of dogs, they were not of his making, sleeping or waking. Their wronged howls surged up from what seemed to be the pit of the earth.

As the sounds of their coming racketed through the rilled and swollen country, Hiram eased the .410 to the pocket of his shoulder and propped his forward arm on his right knee, trying to steady the gun, but as he looked along the barrel the sighting bead made a lazy skate across the valley. When the deer appeared, they burst from the tangles in full flight. Their hides swept past like silverfish. Even their stride was fishlike, haunch and foreleg driving one to the other with a seesawing rhythm as they dodged pulped stumps and stones. Dead branches snapped like a line of musketry.

Hiram did not remember the tension in the trigger or the recoil of the gun. Only the sharp smell of the smoke and his arm going numb.

Within a minute Henry came laboring up the hill. His hat was set on a rakish angle, nearly obscuring his eyes. He stumbled once on an exposed root system, but managed to keep to his feet before coming up short.

"I miss ever blasted thing! Did you hit one?"

"I don't know."

Henry peered over the crest of the ridge. "Well, let's just sit here a minute and then see if they is a blood trail."

When a quarter of an hour had passed, they eased down the hill, searching the twigs and leaves for spots of blood, drawn to it finally by the circling of yellow jackets. It was dark like honey and thick. The boys crouched and watched the woods, mute as a pair of seminarians.

In time, Henry spat and said, "Gut shot." He shook his head. "Best let him bleed out."

Hiram wanted to ask why but knew he was expected to keep silent.

After half an hour they set out on the trail, finding the dark ribboning where the deer had bled heavily at first, moving down a long draw. There they found a clotted pool in some broom sedge where the animal had bedded for a time before breaking for thicker country. When after close to a mile they came panting into a border of laurel, they reached their guns before them like blind men plying their canes, stopping every minute or so to get their bearings in the land that had already swallowed them and now was beginning their slow digestion.

They came finally into a bald blighted strip of mountain bared to the midmorning sun. And on into a firebreak of sifting earth that gave way at their steps. Beyond, they followed the declivity of the northern slope. And still the blood ran, though thinner now, spumey and in jets.

Then it vanished. They had moved down through a forest of large pine and crawling ivy, expecting to find the deer bedded for good beneath a roof of low branches, but as they slowed and watched, nothing revealed itself. They cut a large circle for sign but could find no more blood or pawed dirt. They sat for a while talking and taking their simple breakfast of cold bacon folded between a wedge of corn bread.

"He musta headed toward the river," Henry said. "Can you hear it?"

Hiram strained for the faint echoes of moving water and nodded.

"It's closer than you think. Let's get moving."

They came out of the big pine and into a stony reach of land with small cedars and Spanish bayonet and dried sumac. They smelled the water long before they could see it. The bluffs opened before them, pale and ripped as a broached skullcap. Lichen etched down from the upper rim of palisades across the river and disappeared into the tight mouths of caves that may have been the dens of predators or perhaps only the untenanted pockmarks of swift water erosion.

Henry worked down toward the water first with Hiram a few steps behind, moving stifflegged against the hill and loose stones rolling underfoot. In descent, the noise of the river grew large. The riffles and runs took on new dimensions. Even the deceptively still pools betrayed their eddies and clockwise currents. Once the boys reached the shingle they had to shout to one another to be heard. Henry studied the wet sand for tracks, walking downstream, mindful of hidden fords that might draw them closer to the wounded animal. They saw coon and cat prints but no larger game. They stopped and lowered themselves to the bank, drinking from the white water like beasts themselves. When they rose up, they turned to search the bluffs they had come down into the stony valley.

Hiram saw it first, cubbied on a ledge of grit and holly, tucked in on itself like a whipped dog, the long flat ears pinned back along the antlerless skull. Its eyes were coal black and fixed, seemingly lidless, watching them with almost human regard. Its large nose was wet and its coat ruffled in a passing flit of wind.

When Henry saw the deer he slowly raised his rifle to his shoulder. The moment he laid his cheek along the stock to sight, the doe sprang from its final bedding and clawed for the next higher ledge, tiny rocks clattering over the outcropping like flung dice. Henry's shot went wide to the right, jetting a short cloud of powdered stone. The doe reached the next ledge and once more pinned the ground beneath her front hooves as she tried to lever her rear haunches up, but another climb was too much. Her legs slid out from under the weight of her struggle and she plummeted riverward, striking her ribs against the sharp rocks and brambles, her white tail twirling out behind her before she struck the rapids, the water towing her in the direction of flat rivers where she would bloat and burst under the sun, her meat alive only with parasites.

Hiram and Henry watched her vanish with the current, borne without concession toward the river beyond.

It was Henry who finally said, "We cain't say nothing about this. They like to kill us."

Hiram studied the water for a long time and said, "You're right. There ain't nothing we could say."

Give Up and Go Home, Jasper

Jasper is schooling us on the finer points of fisting. It's only a touch past midnight and he's already managed to lose his camper from betting everything on a Texas Hold 'Em round, praying for a flush that never proved. But now he's on to talking about the love he found for this seventeen year old barmaid after his wife started taking the dick from a Tennessean named Kilowatt, a guy who got his silly ass nickname because he's an electrician, and maybe too, I'm beginning to wonder, because he can deliver a worthy prod. Though this isn't what's bugging Jasper, because Jasper's a plain fool for forgiving his own cuckolding when it comes square up against the magic he says he's found with this girl Janelle and her slender greased digits. Fingers of salvation, is what he calls them, smiling and sweating a little.

This is not a conversation possible without dope and shame. Jasper knows this, and he's helped himself to Jackson's brick of hash. By damn God, if I could catch up with him, but Jackson's only a drinking buddy and not much else, so I'm not about to press my luck with what I've still got wagered on the table. But Jasper's lost in the music of his own speech, and soon enough, all of us are growing bored and mean.

"You mean you make that little ole girl ram her Christian hand up your butt?" This coming from Skintone, his yellow neck bulging from his shirt collar like case meat. "That's Goddamned Godless. I ought to put the law on you, Jasper."

But Jasper will not let the romance be sullied. His eyes leak manly tears. He pleads. Jackson, unimpressed, heads over to the porch fridge and yanks out a pint of chilled vodka and pours out four glasses, setting them down at our open hands.

Now, to appreciate this, you've got to lay eyes on Jasper. He's not a small man, but a soft mountain of toneless matter, skin moist as a worm. And this girl, this Janelle Hicks, is herself no teenage apocalypse. Skinny through the hips with a bad limp. When she comes at you quick, it's spot on for a loosed asylum patient.

"No, no," Jasper hollers through his crying. "These are the truest plights of a good man's heart. No law...no law of nature is broken here."

It is hot, humid for nighttime in the mountains, and the mosquitoes are thumping us something wicked. Jasper was supposed to buy citronella sticks, but he says the store was out. It's possible, I guess. At least he didn't pass up the bag of lemons Skintone demanded, the sucked rinds now sloughed into the ashtray alongside the bashed teeth of unfiltered Camels. That's where Skintone gets his color from, sucking on those grocery store lemons night and day, drawn to them like sin.

Skintone flings his cards on the table, curses us all blind and kisses his vodka. I've never once seen this religious fool so sober and each lick of drink seems only pushes him closer to clarity. We all spend a while sitting and listening for each other's human sounds.

"You know what I have a mind to do," Jackson says, not really talking to any of us. "But to go out and run us a fox."

Skintone snaps his eyes up from his mood. "Shit, how long's it been since you worked them dogs? Four, five months?"

Jackson tips back in his chair, his hands joined over the back strap of his baseball cap, a pose that might just be enough to hold his brains in. "That doesn't have nothing to do with it."

I know we have no choice but to follow once Jackson begins to talk this way. He is our head, our heart, and we amble after his signals like numbed legs. I gather my car keys and billfold in my pocket while Jackson steps around to the backyard where the dogs are already alive and yammering, sensing something in the night air.

"I need to ride with you," Jasper says to me.

"What do you mean, you *need* to?" Skintone spits. He's raging with a deep, sinister calm.

"That's not your concern," Jasper whispers back at him, taking me by the elbow as we walk out toward the edge of the brick hard yard. I can smell dog shit out here somewhere.

I know where Jackson will want to hunt. Spellman Holler, about fifteen minutes outside of town, not far from where the old derelict Sanction County railyard has become a simple steel ache in a history only slightly brighter than this one. It is the place we all go when we go down to forget ourselves and what we lost some place just beyond faithful memory. We go to get drunk and hate one another for being caught alive together in this world and convince ourselves it is all because we love each other like brothers.

There is a steady watershed out there in the holler. Runoff courses the plumbed vertical shale, and after a good rain you can hear the sluice coming down like breathing from the mountains' darkness. It is a kind of joyful death.

The car engine shudders and the valves rattle before the idle eventually roars and steadies. We lurch forward as I spin a wide circle, the CV joints popping like an old man's knees. The night is washed with the vodka and my eyes search the road and the melted sweep of the treeline gusting past. I have my own bottle beneath the seat, and I bubble it twice or more as I drive on. I hear Jasper talking, but the words are queered. Something has fallen from them, defused by the fact of his steady whimpering. I have never heard a grown man cry for so long at a stretch. Of all that I hear, the only sounds that I register are her name and that word that is supposed to mean everything.

"*Love is...is love,*" he moans.

I know this. Every fool does. But true enough, I can see the genius of Jasper in the moment, the reason he is locked in fat flesh and womanish bones. He has conjured something dear from himself and I find him so suddenly beautiful it is hard not to kiss him full on the mouth. The urge is so strong I swerve wide in the bend, kicking gravel high off the shoulder, dinging the bullet riddled octagon of a stop sign. The back end of the car switches for a moment and then runs straight and true once the tires gain traction. We ride. The vodka drains.

Some impulse guides me to the place where I know we will find Jasper's love, stooped over beneath Christmas lights strung from dented wainscoting, hustling neat booze to the late night drunks on a round plastic tray. Her uncle's bar, where she works for nickels and catcalls. To this gloomy keep, we ride. Oh, Janelle, the lover rushes to you, my sweet!

I may be drunk. I may be. I nose into the gravel lot and meet Jasper's amazed eyes.

"Take her, love her," I say. "But hurry up."

Jasper falls out of the car door and cuts his temple on the steel edge, ribboning his skull like a present, but he does not falter. He does not tarry. He careers ahead. Though I stay in the car, my love is with him, carried on his sallow sweating shoulders. In my mind I can see the sedated faces turned towards him, the gaping holes of their voiceless outrage. I can see his wan, female prize, wearing a cocktail apron and blushing coyly beneath her acne, eager to be whisked away to sylvan boughs and a gentle, loving rape.

I am driving again, forgetting them, rolling slowly out when Jasper beats upon the trunk of the car. I remember to stop, letting him and sweet ugly Janelle fling themselves into the back seat, their feet caught and dangling for a moment before I lurch forward and the door swats shut. They make sounds with each other's poor bodies as I drive on toward the holler, the proof of their love delivered in a sharp chemical truth that begins to tell in my nostrils.

When we meet the holler, Jasper and Janelle have righted themselves. I watch them in the rear view mirror as they match buttons and calm their displaced hairs. The car is humid inside.

Skintone and Jackson are already here, getting the dogs out of their kennels. When he sees us, Skintone comes forward with a lemon peel smile, but his words are not friendly.

"What in the hell, Jasper. You bringing jailbait out here, now?"

"Stop your bitching," Jackson says. "Let's get out in the woods."

So we do, moving down towards the treeline with the dogs running forward, eager for scent. We will not follow. That is not the nature of the hunt. Instead, we will build up a fire and put our sweating bodies next to it, heating ourselves to the point of pain because that is what we have always done. Because that is what the fox hunt is. That and listening to the long bays of the dogs as they crash through the distant dark. We will do that and carry our minds through the night after them as they chase the victim to ground. There will be no death, because death would end the trial too soon. Death would interfere with the love of torment, in both the dogs and the men, and that is something no one wants to happen.

Skintone snaps sticks and erects a small temple of kindling for burning. Jackson touches a spurt of flame from his cigarette lighter and we watch as the flame crawls up and begins to live. Soon, bigger deadfall is added, the ugly broken gifts of stormwreck. In time, the dogs cut a scent and start bellowing. Soon, I am lost to the tango of the building fire. The voices cross in the pale pulse where we all sit, but I do not say a word.

The dogs will run the length of the holler. They will run it and be deceived when the fox cuts a clever retreat, but they will run it again, venturing everything to bring the fox to bay. I have always known this because I have been alive forever.

I will not do anything now. I will not stand up to defend the weak when they are assailed. I will remain here, cut to the bone by the nearness of the fire when Skintone reels back and slams the vodka bottle against a stone. He will charge at Jasper, screaming the wrath of Christ to come, the wages of all sins of the flesh descending. He will spit his lemon peel from his jaundiced face, the pure sour triumph as the blood rises. Jackson will look away and listen for the dogs and Janelle will remain small and present, a mere figurine in rags. But I will not do anything now, though I am a defender of love, of the cock and the cunt. I am a defender of all the machinery of happiness. But that will do little to calm Skintone's raging certainty. He is an admirable monster to me. None of us can do anything to stop him as he comes at Jasper, striking savagely with the complete true pleasure of an emptied and righteous heart.

Age of Stone

When McCallister came into the highcountry, old men would come up from distant hollows to watch his crew work the blast lanes and see with their wintered eyes the dreams he carried, see them as clearly as if they were irons slung across the shoulders of the man himself. Some remembered when the railway men had come two generations earlier, siccing their teams of black convicts on the mountains in battalions, picks and sledges bashing through the passes. But 1934 brought a new promise; these men arriving on the ridges held a sheen when the sun touched their bodies. A new word was being spread through the mountains of western North Carolina: *progress.*

In the matter of only a few weeks, the nature of McCallister's mission came to be suspected, and finally affirmed. A tunnel through Callum Mountain, a bold lunatic stroke clean through the granite wedge at the east end of Croptop Gorge. They were to rip open a gate to plunge down into the gorge so that the WPA men could pave the road through, opening up the world to the hillcountry and the hillcountry to it.

At first, the young men of the county did nothing. They did not trust McCallister because he wore knee high boots buffed to a high military polish and kept a severe manner, even in his few dealings with the store keeps and suppliers of the closest town of any size, Canon City, a riverbound settlement of less than two thousand Scots-Irish souls. But the notion of jobs wormed its way into them, especially at the first gnaw of autumn cold. They knew the deep hurt of winter would be on their families soon and any man who turned down work was not only a fool, but a traitor to his kin because no good son would inflict needless hardship on those who claimed him as their only shield against that ancient anguish, Old Age.

So they had come up to the ridge, singly and in small speechless knots, hands rammed into their pockets as they watched McCallister's specialists trudge the stony path down towards the tunnel blasting. For some time the mountain boys had been content to merely watch, to place themselves in the sight of these outsiders. But when nothing had come of the simple assertion of their attendance, they began to sling canvas lean-tos from hickory branches and assemble around firepits leaking cheerless runnels of cook smoke. They whet knives against small bricks of flint. Their eyes perched tightly in bowed skulls.

McCallister ignored them for most of October, but by the month's end he made their number close to thirty and he knew some measure must be taken. He resolved to drive them off and rode out to the encampment on his black Arabian, a horse a full seventeen hands high. A Colt revolver stuck through his whipcord belt.

He explained to them the danger of the operation he and his men were engaged in and warned that no ground in the area could be construed as hazardless. Their attack on the mountain was a relentless demand of exact science, he said, but it must be remembered that the weight of stone obeyed its own law of destruction. The ways of men were nothing in the face of such naked power. Workers who lacked the advantage of training and a particular education were as good as dead if they ventured into the growing blast lanes. In good conscience, he would not hire any man into his own oblivion. He thought this warning would be enough to repulse them, to drive them back to their coves and crags, and if not the words alone then the thump and pulse through the ground when a large charge detonated at the conclusion of his speech, clouds of powdered stone rising from below like haints absenting the tomb.

But the young men had remained there, crouching and spectating from within the boundaries of their makeshift assembly, overnighting as they had for those preceding weeks, talking to one another in the hard twang of highcountry natives, a murmured language that snaked through vowels long and pliable as field weeds.

So McCallister's only recourse had been simple. He had taken the company truck to the county seat of Canon City and stood inside the empty hallways of the courthouse, waiting with his hat in his hands to be granted audience with the High Sheriff. He was prepared to pay the law its due, to pacify the locals with these formalities. McCallister understood that a certain brand of man could not be warned away by the exercise of logical appeal, that an application of legal intimidation was necessary. He had dealt with similar problems in

Central America. He considered it an eccentricity of hermetic peoples, this insolence in the face of development. Something in these sequestered populations seemed incapable of comprehending the onset of a larger history, of forward movement. Of all the elements of the world he was proud to claim as his foe, none was a greater enemy to him than barbarism.

When he returned to the Callum Mountain work site, he was not alone. Three armed deputies and the High Sheriff himself accompanied him. They leaned on their Springfield rifles and discussed the nature of the winter to come with the loafing boys, speaking not in direct threats but in that vague suggestive tone that said more than any sharp word ever could.

Leave these Yankees to their work, boys, the High Sheriff said. It'll run a true course in good time.

Within half an hour the trespassers had bundled their few wares and marched off the ridge, tramping back sullenly to their remote cabins and homeplaces, a company of the dispossessed hurrying on to a cold hearth and the colder certainty of family heartbreak. McCallister watched them go.

Once the law men had lingered well into the afternoon to make sure none of the local boys came back, they returned to Canon City. As they drove away, McCallister sent word down to the tunnel to cease work early for the day. That evening a cask of whiskey was broached and several chickens were slaughtered and roasted over open fires. Late into the night the laborers hunched over these gifts, growing drunk and food bloated beneath a cooling moon, the marginal, half-serious rivalries inherent in men long in the field together giving way to easy conversations and low stakes gambling.

McCallister himself went among them, these men who were closer to him than his own family. From somewhere a stool was retrieved and he settled himself to it, picking up a hand of cards dealt on the anvil flat surface of a tree stump. Bets circled and chips were tossed, rattling amid the congenial laughter. McCallister drew his cards close to his breast and shifted forward to gain the benefit of the coal-oil lantern when the card suddenly snapped from his hand, torn from his fingers with some phantom energy, the whistle and crack of the report following hard on. When one of the men discovered the card lying some several feet away, the Queen of Spades had been perforated with a .22 slug, neatly punched between heart and head.

Two men decamped that first week, claiming the elevation to be bad for their lungs. McCallister paid them for their services without interrogation. They were good hands, but none that could not be replaced. Anyone who would be driven from their destiny by a few stray snipings was not one McCallister could long hold in his esteem. He drove them himself to the train station in one of the company cars and turned back without a single word of regret. On the way back he posted a travel request to a pair of skilled blast technicians in Maryland. A week later these two replacements were drilling in the tunnel. The pit in the mountain continued to engorge.

In the evenings at the end of the week when they were not disposed to the work in the tunnel, the men would wash themselves in long zinc troughs and dress in broadcloth suits and banded hats before piling into the company's trucks for the hour ride to Asheville. They enjoyed the addictions of men who had seen some fair portion of the world, who possessed a greater appetite than could be easily satisfied between the great walls of the Great Smokeys and Blue Ridge. McCallister encouraged this appreciation in them. As someone who had visited the darker corners of the world, he made it a point not to employ men without some sense of sophistication. There was some great truth in this, he thought, some testament to the essential fabric of the work they were doing if it was done by men who understood the finer principles of a fully lived life.

But despite their revels, the men would always return before daybreak of the following Monday morning, not a single one of them with an exploded collar or bloodshot eyes because McCallister would not tolerate a drunkard among his crew. In this he was religious. Weekly, he would remind them that the tunnel was their great whore, the one in which they were privileged to share, and only by otherwise living above moral reproach would they be granted the gift of returning to her.

In December, the old sickness came on McCallister and he spent several sleepless nights battling fever, only to rise the following mornings with the internal heat gone but still cursed with a body in pure revolt, pouring every nourishment from him as soon as it entered. He knew it to be the price he had paid for his many expeditions, the legacy of foreign diseases only partially dispelled. As he lay wrestling among his swaddle of wool blankets he would try to search his memory for what place or time had infected him with this recurrent suffering, but it was impossible. There were too many murky cups of tea, too many foul reservoirs upwind of jungle encampments. But the worst of the burden wasn't in the physical pain alone. That could be borne well enough, shouldered as part of some due necessity. Instead, it was the accompanying fear that his life could end with tasks left undone, a project untidily finished, that troubled him most.

His only consolation was the predictable percussions of blasting that went on despite his absence from the site. The work had progressed deep enough into the mountain that it took on an energy and will of its own. His second in command, Waynewright, brought him reports twice daily, morning and evening. But the hard numbers of feet gained and the diameter of enlargement did not interest McCallister. No, he could feel the accomplishment of violence through the earth when it shook beneath him.

Then a deadly shot was fired. Late afternoon on one of the approaching ridges, skylined, the men moved down towards the tunnel like iron targets set on pickets. A crack of the rifle. Waynewright himself was shot through the throat, pitching headfirst from the ridge, uttering not a syllable as he fell. The company scrambled and grasped at their pioneering gear as they pursued the few retreating bushwhackers exposed across the gorge, the blast technicians lacking the advantage of modern arms but compelled now by the argument of blood and loss. With ax and pick and hammer, McCallister's men reared bellowing from the assault with single-minded fury, striking out over the rockscape like men loosed for fatal reckonings.

When the news of murder was delivered, McCallister rose immediately from his fever bed and had the Arabian saddled and bridled, his Army Springfield strapped to its flank. The fire of sickness burned in his face so strongly that it colored him with a false appearance of bucolic health but a true tell of his outrage. McCallister's risen temper was such that even men who would have called him brother in years past did not dare risk the slightest disfavor for fear of the penalty the man might enact. In that moment, he did not invite the look of one who knew the word Mercy.

The bushwhackers, in their haste, had left a clear trail. With only the best and furious trailing him, McCallister silently followed the criminal tracks. Once night had overtaken him, he dismounted and followed on foot, guided by the feeble moon and the imprudent sounds coming from where the bushwhackers had made camp in the lee of stone bluffs. He could see their fires burning in bright whirling pools below. Their diminished shapes passed like shadow tricks against the muted flames. The idea, the recrimination, took shape somewhere in that distant space of cold light and infinite blackness.

He sent three of his blast technicians back to the tunnel, warning them to steal as quietly to their munitions and to bear them back to him as fast as they could. Crouched there, gazing over the precipice, he waited as the wheeling galaxy spun itself above him in its inevitable regularity, blind to the world below it.

The men returned within the hour, humped over with explosives. McCallister gently took these bundles diapered in tight butcher paper, figuring amounts of dynamite with his own hands, knowing there was an intelligence in joints and flesh as much as mind, the law of touch to be trusted now above any mathematical prescription. The placement must be perfect in order to coordinate the blast. The divisions were made. Four separations divvied out to the men, leaving the largest central placement to McCallister himself. With final words of luck, they each slipped over the edge and down the face of the cliff, cleaving to the dark edge of the world as they lowered themselves into position.

McCallister's descent was made in silence and he could hear no more than the slightest shift of kicked gravel as his men set their charges nearby. This simple sound alone was all he needed. The plan was well devised, well bent towards its end. The stone, he knew, desired to kill. Once the separate fuses had been run back and linked at the crest of the overlook, and all men accounted for at the top, McCallister squatted down and touched the flame to the wire. The fire's slow movement spent itself along the fuses and over the edge in a scrim of smoke a moment before it met the charges and the earth recoiled.

Three days lapsed before news of the blasting's true effect reached them, and then it was only from the mouths of the grieving women. They came like creatures dragged whole out of the valley itself, enough to make a camp in their own right. Stiffbacked and shawled, they bore themselves to him without tears, mountain proud, asking the work on the tunnel be ceased for the day while they did rites for their lost kin. The burying had already been done by the earth itself. Only then did McCallister learn the men at the base of the cliffs had numbered but two, the rest of the bushwhackers having moved into the next valley, escaping unknown into the wider country. The others, the seven, were camp boys left behind. And there had been an eighth, a little girl who had tagged along, anxious for her brother's safety. She too among them. These simple tenders of cookwares and builders of evening fires had been smashed and lost forever beneath the weight of the broken bluffs.

McCallister gave his consent to the work suspension and retired to his windy tent, receiving no reports or requests while he took to his cot for the rest of the day, occasionally leaning from the edge of his cot and vomiting quietly onto the ground. Some men thought they heard him pray that night, though none could be sure.

Shortly thereafter, he began to suffer the harassment of the frozen night airs. A disturbance that was hard to locate or define, but one that corrupted sleep. If these nights could be given certain character, then it was in the late hour's saddened presence, working on McCallister's mind like boot blacking. A distress that lacked definition had set its jaws, tightening around him as the long evenings went hard without rest.

Then, in their stricken and sundered forms, the children began appearing to him.

For many nights he counted their figures as mere apparitions, ghosts of conscience whom he could not seal from waking sight. But unlike spirits, their bodies persisted in a gorish physical state. Their decay smelled and when they moved they left behind a thin scrawl of blood. One, an animated trunk, carried his severed head inside a brown canvas poke. Another, a girl with braids, wore a sliver of shale in place of a necklace, impaled on one side at the collarbone and jutting diagonally down into her slim body. The stained tip at the other end emerged from her back, just above the lowest bump of her rent vertebrae.

The dead would not enter McCallister's tent, but would congregate by the patches of moonlight in the clearings, drawn to that silvering in death as living men might seek the comfort of a mended fire. Whenever he tried to sleep he could hear the quieted grinding of their bones.

With lantern and pistol he went out to them and watched their aimless trudge, growing so sick in body he felt he was no better than a matured figure of their own woe. He lifted his pistol, and at once they turned, fixing him where he stood, the strength of his trigger finger lost. Fatigue washed him pale, and he knew then that every man is hapless in his dreams. He returned to his tent.

The following days offered poor consolation for McCallister. The winter rock deep in the tunnel was unmanageable. Blasting dimensions varied wildly despite the exactness of the laid charges. Some spoke of seams of stubborn mineral, but often the detonation would cause far greater wreck to the stone than expected. Nothing could be reliably predicted. Physics had somehow managed to fail. Men known as fearless began to develop nerves. Two more disappeared, but this time no effort was made to find replacements.

In January an uncommon blizzard stormed through the highcountry, restricting the entire working crew to camp three days running. The only movement at night was the workers hustling between the high, flashing fires, and McCallister watched their colorless forms chase across the flames. Their appearance was oddly frightening, inhuman. The automated movement of life but without character or intelligence. Upright beasts only. Mere machines of survival.

Only when the fires smoldered and the men retired did the children come, dragging their broken limbs through the drifts. Their teeth chattered. Their blood burned smoking trails. McCallister called softly to them, begging their absence, but if they heard they did not obey. He cried out, damning them, but that, he feared, had already been done.

He ran barefoot from his tent and directly to the supply shed, levering a shovel handle against the drift sealed door, cracking in finally. The children turned to watch him.

And quickly now, his numbed legs pistons in the snow, the sacks of charges slung forward from his shoulders and over his belly, a clumsy pregnancy as he held the canvas tight at its throat so that none of the dynamite might be lost. And quickly to the tunnel, the sealed space where the work had once been its own fulfilled appetite. A difference now, a fatal difference decided by something beyond McCallister, and for that it should be crippled.

He handed the charges out to the children and watched as they set the dynamite into the drilled holes, the honeycombed face filling with the papered sticks. The largest bundles he placed himself, and he made certain that it was ready before he called the children to his side. They surrounded and embraced him like his own.

The fuse was quick. The mountain and every blow he had delivered against it came down. McCallister alone opened his arms in welcome.

Confederates

I knew I spoke out of turn when I asked my father's old friend Charlie Jobe what he thought would come of moving to the veterans' camp, or "Village of the Deranged," as the newspaper has since taken to calling it. That was their description after all the trouble with the State Police. At the time, though, it seemed to me nothing more than a gathering of old drunks and madmen living out of tents and plyboard hovels. For Charlie, though, it was something else.

"It takes guts," he said, thumbing his middle. "Guts and a three thousand dollar community lien."

"Community lien?" I asked, not hiding my suspicion.

He swatted at my words like they were a cloud of no-see-ums.

"That's what they call it. I'm not particular about their legal doings. It's over there in Seneca, in South Carolina. They had it on the evening news just last night."

Charlie leaned back in his metal folding chair, balancing his weight with the one good foot pressed flat against the pine slatted floor, the same floor I helped him cobble together from shipping pallets we stole one midnight a couple of falls back from the loading dock behind Lowe's.

"Listen to me," he tipped his head with intent, his skull harrowing from crown to brow.

"I'm listening."

"Your daddy would understand what I'm saying."

Thereby he conjured up the old ghost, and I knew I was in for one hell of a long afternoon if I didn't keep the conversation moving.

"Where are you going to get three thousand dollars?" I asked, knowing I would surely cringe at the answer.

He cleared his throat and looked off at the side yard, a little graveyard of rusted engine blocks and mechanical doodads. He once made a living swapping automobile parts for groceries or booze with the local hillfolk.

"I was hoping you could give me a ride down to Cherokee," he said, lifting his chin a little and squinting at the sun, wearing his cracked mask of wounded pride.

"Cherokee?" I asked. "What's in Cherokee that has anything to do with three thousand dollars?"

As soon as the question was out of my mouth, I knew what he had in mind.

The casino.

"I got my VA disability check just yesterday," he said, patting his prosthesis, as if he could sound out the value of his lost limb with that hollow little whack. It was the same leg he used to remove at night and then dangle above my head on late mornings when I'd overslept at the deer camp. You can believe it worked. There are few things in this world more effective at getting you out of the bed than a levitating limb sporting a jungle boot.

There was no reasoning with him now. His mind was committed, and I realized I had no earthly choice but to help my father's dear friend.

We left early Friday afternoon because my painting job cut loose sooner than I'd been led to believe. I had a change of clothes in a black duffel in the back of the cab, but Charlie stumped out and rattled his stick against the Chevy's door while the engine was still running, the valves rattling.

"Come on, we can still beat the rush. They's plenty truckstops where you can change and clean up."

I considered explaining stopping now or later amounted to the same thing, but he toppled in and beat the dash with the flat of his palm, urging the pick up on like it was a slow mule. I hauled the transmission down to Drive and eased out onto the road to the white hot sounds of popping gravel. Charlie's grin was as wide as greed itself.

Once we were on the highway, he rifled through the glove box, filing through my uncased cassettes, kissing his teeth when he came across something he considered worthwhile. He lingered over my Woody Guthrie, my Kris Kristopherson, my Cash. One radio speaker was out, so he had to wrench the silver knob all the way around until the guitar and breath rasped and squawked from the perforations in the passenger side door. He hummed along, shaping his mouth to the words he strained to recall.

For some reason, his singing reminded me of the old times with Dad and him, spitting rocks and dust on dirtbikes, scrabbling all over Kingdom Come looking for signs of game—tracks or scat. Charlie and my Dad a pair to behold, crippled up Vietnam geezers roaring through the woods motocross style with me suckered against one of their backs like some tumor realized full with hair and eyeballs. The motors huffing and screaming over my pleas and each of them laughing like redneck devils on holiday from hell.

Things started to go wrong just outside of Sylva. The tape deck choked. "The Night They Drove Old Dixie Down" wrung up bad, stretching out Robbie Robertson's voice like some runaway child put to the rack. Charlie nearly went through the windshield with rage.

"Goddamn outdated..."

Once he managed to recover, he removed the tape, fiddled and frowned.

"You need to upgrade to CDs. This is trash."

He cradled the slack amber tape on the tips of his index and middle fingers while carefully winding the plastic spool with the soft motor of his pinky. The tangle refused to budge and he flung it back in the glove compartment, drawing out an old Skynyrd instead. "Free Bird" soared.

It wasn't long before he had to pee. There was nothing along the way but river guide services advertising that the indoor restrooms were for paying customers only. Normally, Charlie'd drop trou on the side of the road, but the traffic was picking up and he worried about piss blowback from the vehicles whipping by.

Down the way, we found a place. I parked and followed Charlie inside a tourist shop with my small duffel slung over my shoulder. The on-duty clerk eyed me intently as I walked back, figuring me a threat to his vast collection of flamingos, Lincoln Logs, water pistols, books on tape and imitation headdresses. I gave him the finger for no reason in particular.

The restroom was a small partionless square with a single working toilet and anonymous stains and biological splatters. The smell was like the inside of a hospice. While Charlie leaned over the commode, I turned to the wall and stripped out of my working coveralls, changing into jeans and a tee shirt. I sealed my dirty work clothes with a single sharp zip.

The toilet flushed and Charlie came out to run water over his hands.

"You sure about this, Charlie?" I asked. "Your whole check, I mean, that's a lot of fucking money..."

His eyes met mine in the mirror, suddenly making me ten years old again. That was that.

Once back on the highway, Charlie decided to forsake the tape deck for a shitkicker station out of Knoxville. The signal was too weak, though, and he soon shut it off.

"You're a stupid sonofabitch, you know that?" he said. "Ticking off that clerk for no good reason."

He shook his head and let his hand slip outside the window, catching air. Heat and humidity batted at us like a pair of slow children.

"How long are you gonna go on living like this?"

I had known this was coming, dammit, but here it was.

"Like what, Charlie?"

"Like every other hardhead in that family of yours. I swear to God. I'll never understand it. More wasted brains than the devil would ever need. You painting houses for a living, with the education you got. Goddamn waste. Boy like you living like he was born in a cage."

He reared up on one cheek and drew a glass maple syrup bottle from his cargo pocket. I smelled the whiskey as soon as he unscrewed the black cap and took a nip.

"What happened to that flask I got you at Christmastime?" I asked, trying to turn him aside from the road he meant to take.

He shrugged, not giving in.

"Now you know I loved your daddy, boy. More than if he were my own brother. But he'd be a sorry sight to behold if he were here to see you following down that same way that took him."

I wrapped my fingers tight to the heavy dial of the steering wheel, thinking before I said anything. I knew the story Charlie had planned for me already. It was family history, well-known and overworn. My father, Thomas Hilliard, the best of his kin, come back from Vietnam and gone to Emory on the GI Bill. A self-made man, the whole world spread before him like a Technicolor dream....before drink and pills set him up in a motel room where he painted his brains on the bathroom tile with a 12 gauge Mossberg pump gun.

"It's not an easy thing to live with, Charlie."

He sipped.

"Hell, boy, I know that."

Charlie knew I'd been out of Copestone asylum for nearly six months. Sanity by pills and needles was by now a distant, nostalgic memory. For so long it had been only the serrated edge of getting by from one day to the next. Not because Daddy was gone, but because I was the one left behind to deal with his going. That and those feelings were still as attached to me as my own complexion.

"Eye color ain't the only thing he passed on, you know?"

Charlie nodded but said nothing.

After a while he waved the whiskey bottle over at me and I took it, drinking a little but letting most run back down from my tongue in backwash. I'd spent one night in jail with a DUI and knew better than to hazard another run-in with state troopers.

I let my hands lose themselves in the steering wheel, riding the deep curves of the drive. For the moment, I was happy in the simple mechanics of eating up road, guiding the big truck through the boundaries of the lane, and only a little afraid. The green wash of passing scenery stung my eyes and my conscience, but I managed to let go of as much of that as I could.

It was Charlie that saw them first; I was still lost somewhere in the fog of my thoughts. He leaned forward beside me, his seatbelt clicking in its retractor as he strained against the harness, tapping his stick against the windshield.

"Lord awmighty."

I registered the words and was aware of humped shapes on the highway's shoulder, but I did not slow down. Memory was weighting the accelerator. I did not slow until one of the soldiers, waving his foraging cap from the jagging bayonet of his musket, ripped me back to the moment.

Dust and rocks flew up, ticking off the undercarriage from a swerve made too fast, the rear wheels mired for a split second as we fishtailed into a halt. We sat rocking without saying anything, then I swiped the lever up a notch to Reverse and pulled back to the slumped Mercedes.

The Rebels had blown their right rear tire. They stood there, fists on hips and grey woolen tunics splayed from their pale breastbones like dressed bream. They smiled through their whiskers while the single bald faced one among them, the one that flagged us down, hopped in his cavalry boots, coming up along the edge of the macadam.

"I should stick that damn thing through your guts," I said, pointing to the covered tip of the bayonet. Looking up at the point where his cap dangled, he smiled, mistaking me for someone in a good mood. Charlie smacked me on the chest, a warning to shut up.

"Where you boys headed?" Charlie called good naturedly, trying on the easy conversationalism of country people like a Goodwill suit.

They told us they belonged to a group of reenactors that went by the name "Lee's Miserables" and that they were headed up a little above the reservation to shoot empty powder charges across the Oconaluftee River at their Yankee brethren. Provided they found a way to change their flat on time, of course.

A spare lay in the ditch while one of the confederates wound the thin lever on the jack. The problem was with the jack itself. It was black with a housing as slim as a bullet. As the Mercedes gently rose, the angle of the roadside worked at the base so that it lost its grip and rolled forward, settling the car back on the dirt. Their jack, simply put, was feeble.

I went back to the truck to drag out my gear while Charlie asked one of them for a cigarette and started talking and smoking with the rest. When I came back with the truck jack and my tire iron, I slung everything down there next to a roadkill crushed copperhead that was a flat imprint on the asphalt. The snake looked like something you'd see in a cartoon for the Road Runner to come and scoop up with a spatula. The soldier with the ballistic jack sidled off.

While I positioned the big spoon of the truck jack and put the tire iron on the nuts to break the torque, part of me listened to what Charlie and the confederates were talking about. He said how he admired men that would take time out of their lives to preserve the rites of history, how that meant something given the madness of the contemporary world. He asked if any of them had been veterans themselves. Only one said that he had, but it had been back in the eighties and he'd spent his enlistment sitting in a barracks in Düsseldorf, waiting for weekend liberty when he could spend his pay on "whatever dirty German bitch would blow me." I could see that he felt bad after he said this. His face was pinched and a little bloodless. The others were all college graduates. Professional men. I think one of them even worked at a bank.

They looked on while I laid the iron down and pumped the lever so that the Mercedes rose. The car alarm screamed. All of them went crazy patting their britches to see who had the keys. It was the flagman who'd left them on the hood. He tapped the little deactivate button so that I could get on and get this business done for them.

Once the tire was changed and I'd put my tools back in the Chevy's paint splattered bed, one of the confederates held out a fifty dollar bill to me.

I said he didn't need to bother.

"Come on, now. Take it. Don't make me feel bad."

Grant's foggy portrait riffled in the wind.

"How about a cold beer instead."

The confederate shrugged and went back to the trunk of his car. We all popped cans of Heineken, sucked them down and tossed the dead soldiers in the ditch.

Charlie said it was time to saddle up and leave these boys to their war-fighting. I had nothing there keeping me, so I was as ready to go as any man alive. We sat and watched them ease onto the highway and take off with a high hard toot of their horn, the sunlight a strange halo on their tinted sunroof.

I pulled on the highway and gunned it. We were to the casino in another ten minutes.

Charlie struck it on loose slots that night. A silver river of money poured out onto the puke green carpet. The casino had to bring the security guards out to make sure nobody ran in and started stuffing it into their purses and fanny packs.

Once Charlie moved down to Seneca, he had me bolt together some particle board around a used camper he'd set next to a muddy hole in the ground he called a fishing pond. He claimed he was happy there with all the old coots, plinking at squirrels and living a free life, a life "without legal attachments" he called it. When the government came in about the camp's taxes, Charlie was one of the ones most loyal to the leader of the whole thing. He wouldn't give up his spot no matter what. I swear I can't remember the old bastard's name who ran the place, who started the trouble. Regardless, when the rifles started cracking, Charlie was somewhere in the midst of it all, holed up in one of the outbuildings, answering police snipers with his lever action .22. He may have been one of the ones that killed that trooper out of Greenville, but there's no telling, not with the crossfire the newspapers described. But what I keep wanting to know is what Charlie was thinking while he was pinned there in that shack, the rounds ticking off the aluminum sides. What dream of freedom made him and those like him so different from all the rest of us?

A World of Daylight

Packer came home on Good Friday, watching April rain stripe the green chickenwire window of the empty Greyhound terminal, knowing that by Easter morning he would be putting his brother's killer in the ground. The bad weather had gotten into his head somewhere between the bus ride between Lexington and Asheville. The feeling flooded him, welling up until there was a kind of infected softness behind his eyes, swollen like hot blisters. He moved his head as if afraid it might crack and fizz. He hadn't been drinking, but wished he had. A desire for oblivion he would meet soon, but not until he'd found Drema Chase, convinced himself she wasn't some phantom of his own making, but a receipt of hate he could grasp.

Shirttail met him at the wet curb, the Bronco still running with that pneumatic chug from years ago. Packer walked around to the back and swung open the gate to stow his bags.

"Smells like shit back here, Cousin."

Shirttail seemed to have read a compliment in this. He was grinning when Packer came back around and got in.

"Maybe it's the company," Shirttail said, laughing and lighting a cigarette. He waved the match out, bleeding a current of smoke through the driver's cracked window. Once he had the cigarette drawing, he leaned up hard on the steering wheel and turned onto the access road, not looking either way.

Almost immediately, they entered the mountainside tunnel, the granite heart inside smooth and deep, the hiss of rain giving way to memory. Packer rested his head back on the seat and closed his eyes, letting go. Inside him, a passage opened and he could picture Drema when he'd last seen her and his brother Cab together, shortly after Packer had gotten back from Iraq. There had been a relative's wedding, a barbecue reception somewhere down around Waynesville. Grills and smoke and badly behaved children reputed to be distant kin. But what Packer remembered best was the way Drema circled her slim, needful arm around Cab's waist, the urgent static she seemed to give off, as if the love in the flesh she could give his brother could make up for everything else she couldn't. Packer opened his eyes to the crush of muted light as they came through the tunnel. Reaching down, he traced the shape of the snub-nosed pistol strapped tight against his inner ankle.

"You got the address?"

"It ain't changed," Shirttail said, not taking his eyes off the road. The city was an emptiness around it.

"You're still with me on this, aren't you, Cousin?"

Shirttail said nothing, only looked at him. Packer decided that meant he had nothing to worry about.

They sat in the Bronco at the bottom of the hill behind a screen of knit kudzu, watching Drema's trailer, its tiny plastic windows as neat as pieces missing from a puzzle.

After a while Shirttail said, "Well, let's get on for godssake. It's nothing that can be done in the daytime."

When Packer said nothing, Shirttail cranked the engine and eased back out to the hardtop, waiting for a lone semi to roar past before turning out.

Packer felt tiredness come on him suddenly. He must have drifted off into a light sleep for a time because the road seemed to glide away from him when he closed his eyes, but when he heard the slowing tires and the sound of pool balls snapping, he knew Shirttail had taken him on an unscheduled stop. The faint red strobe on his eyelids told him exactly where.

"What's this?" he asked, his eyes still closed.

"Look, I know you and him have bad blood, but he's on your side on this. You need somebody who can watch your back."

Packer slumped forward. "I thought that's what you were supposed to be for."

"Just talk to the man, will you? Shit, beer's on me."

Without waiting to see if Packer would follow, Shirttail hauled himself out of the Bronco and went through the open front door of Mackey's. Packer hadn't stepped foot inside his stepfather's place in more than seven years, the last time just after his Mama's funeral. Through the glass facade, Packer could see maybe a dozen men in caps and jeans inside, milling around a pair of coin fed billiard tables. After a long minute, he went in.

Tim McGraw and Faith Hill were on the jukebox, wheedling at one another about how their true love would never die. Packer walked past the idle racket, nodded to a few of the familiar faces and drew up a stool next to Shirttail at the far end of the bar. An uncapped bottle of Bud was already set before him. He stared in at the shelves of booze stacked row upon row, each of his multiple reflections distended in the tricked turns of the bottle shapes.

"You wouldn't have thought to ask if I would agree to this?" Packer asked, tilting back the beer, draining it below the label before setting the longneck back on the bar.

Before Shirttail could answer, Packer felt a wide palm spread across his shoulder blades.

"It's been a while," Mackey said in his ear.

Packer turned his head over his shoulder and jerked a nod. "Kentucky to Carolina is a long pull."

A beat too long. "No it ain't. Why don't you two step on back to the office with me?"

They swiped their beers from the counter and followed Mackey back. On the way, Packer glanced over to where a few guys were throwing darts. A tall blond man with a handlebar mustache threw a bullseye. To celebrate, he tossed off half a pilsner glass of beer, then bit down a full inch on the rim, the glass crunching in his mouth as he chewed and swallowed. All of his friends laughed.

Once they reached the blind end of the hall, Packer leaned into the office. A banker's lamp cast an aquatic green glow on the couch and chairs, mere suggestions of shape. The three men moved back towards the white pool of direct lamplight, navigating by the sound of their footsteps alone. Packer remembered how as a child he could see the impossible largeness of falling black space the moment he closed his eyes before sleep. The runaway dimensions of his surroundings would make him believe that, just for a moment, his mind had turned to smoke and filled every corner of the room.

Mackey sat down behind the old desk. Packer and Shirttail dropped into the deep cushioned sofa opposite.

"So you mean to kill her, huh?" Mackey's voice sounded like it came from the long end of nowhere.

Packer turned his head towards Shirttail's silhouette.

"I guess this ain't a town for secrets."

Mackey waved his hand at Shirttail. "It's none of his fault. He's worried about you. Don't be so goddamn hard-headed."

Packer crushed his pockets for nonexistent smokes. Mackey shook out a Winston and lit it for him.

"Don't think I'm trying to stop you," Mackey said. "Cab was my own boy. I know that might not mean much to you, Pack, but it sure as hell does to me."

Packer could not see Mackey's eyes. He never trusted the man, not since he'd stepped into his life when his Mama came home from Jellico, Tennessee with a dime store wedding band choking her finger and a scrawny boy sitting out at the curb, too shy to come inside the house.

"This is your new Daddy and brother," she had said, drawing that skin mask of hers into tight smile lines, hard and sharp enough to cut cardboard.

The resentment for Mackey had come easily and true, but there had been something in Cab, something in the discovered boy that mended itself to Packer. Brothers first, then friends. And now, that little shy boy all those years ago grown up only to find the other side of the ground because his woman had gotten him killed over a bad meth score. Money miscounted and weapons drawn and a poor, foolish life ripped out of a poor fool's body.

"What you holding?" Mackey asked.

Packer looked up and unsnapped the ankle holster, handing the pistol across. Mackey dandled the Smith and Wesson in one flat palm, then placed it to the other, weighing the handgun a moment before passing it back.

"That should definitely get the job done. Kill the cunt good. I'll talk to people, make sure they saw you sitting in here when it gets done. Least I can do, I guess."

"What about the tweaker? The one who pulled the trigger that put Cab in the ground?"

"Been taken care of," Mackey answered, hacking into his hands, the deep chest rattle of cigarette smoke a painful voice inside him. "They didn't even bother dragging the river. Question is, is if you've got the stomach for killing her. She was your woman before she was his, after all."

Packer holstered the snubnose and dropped his trouser cuff in place. Was this one of the necessary plagues on his own heart? To do this thing, to take Drema out of this world, but to do so with complete love. What could be left after that?

"Lord, Mack. Why is it you think I'm the one what

wants to do it?"

Packer dropped Shirttail off at his trailer, refusing his company but taking the Bronco and bottle of bonded bourbon.

"Shit, this can leave 'til tomorrow, Pack. You need to come on up with me to my Mama's place and drink some fucking strawberry wine. Think about this. This isn't something that can be done alone. This is the Lord's weekend, for God's sake."

Packer swung the door shut. "I'll be back in the morning, Cousin. Don't sit up for me."

Before Shirttail could say anything, Packer was gone.

He did not take the direct way up to Drema's. Instead, he drove down through the emptied streets, all the good men and women of the world behaving themselves this sacred weekend of Christ's suffering. Without meaning to or making any deliberate plan of which he was aware, he turned up the Blue Ridge Parkway and drove out along the scenic ridges, watching the serene lights of the city, pulling over finally at one of the overlooks where he could hear a watershed in the darkness. He cracked the cap on the bonded bourbon and drank it in a slow pull until he felt a warm tide lap up from his toes.

"The blood of the lamb," he whispered, toasting the night.

This would be the place to take her. It revealed itself to him like the cold logic of a dissection. All of the bare truth of life reduced to crudely functioning parts. That's what this place was for Drema and him—the simple bones of fate.

The drive over to Drema's place was not far. He

parked at the edge of the paved road and walked up, carrying the bourbon under his arm. By the time he had climbed the stairs to the deck and knocked, he had nearly forgotten the weight haltering his ankle. He could hear a TV running inside loud, but no footsteps. He knocked again.

A little tow headed boy answered the door. He was about as big around as a fencepost.

"Drema in there?" Packer asked.

The boy plucked a green sucker out of one grimy corner of his mouth, switched it to the other and tamped it back in place, eying Packer. "She lives here, but she's out right now."

"Out?"

"That's right."

Packer tried to get a look inside, but could make out nothing.

"I know she doesn't have a kid. Sure enough not one big as you."

"I didn't say I was hers, did I? My daddy and her were friends."

"Were? Not still?"

Packer guessed the boy to be around ten, but it was hard to tell. He looked like nothing so much as an animate skeleton wearing a costume of tightened skin.

"I'm gonna come in and sit down and wait on her, then. And you ain't gonna do anything about it, okay?"

The boy stumbled aside, letting the hollow wooden door swing open as he pounded back to the kitchen. The whole trailer shook. Packer went over, switched the TV off and made room between magazines and a pile of clothes for a place to sit on the couch.

Everything smelled sour.

"I'll call the law on you, asshole," the boy said, lifting the phone receiver from its plastic cradle. Packer could see that no line ran to the wall.

"Settle down, I'm not doing anything but waiting on Drema."

The boy returned the useless phone to its place, but he did not take his eyes from Packer nor venture a step closer. For a while, they watched each other.

"I used to live around here, you know," Packer said, uncapping the bourbon.

The boy tossed his head to rid his eyes of dirty bangs.

"You ain't a pervert, are you?"

"Just relax, Chief. Go look at some comic books or something."

The boy did not move.

"You're not supposed to just walk into somebody else's house like this. It ain't right."

"Hush now."

"It's true."

Under the TV a slick black Playstation console buzzed. Packer felt ugly under the boy's gaze.

"You want to play a game on the tube until she gets here? Hell, it'll give you a chance to whoop my ass."

The boy did not answer but tossed one of the video game controllers to Packer while he punched in a series of menu commands on the remote control until the television slashed on and a desert battlefield appeared. The boy pushed buttons again and the screen bisected horizontally so that each of the players hunted the other with an assault rifle and grenades. Packer tried to use what he knew about tactics, proper cover and concealment and ambush positions, but the action was too hectic. The boy's avatar zigzagged impossibly, drawing close and firing into Packer's face before he could get a clean shot. The score grew lopsided and the boy became bored and said he was done playing.

Packer looked round at the thin walls, the displaced knickknacks on the pressboard shelves and on the shag carpet. His eye fell on something he'd given Drema years ago sitting on the mantle piece. A plastic egg no bigger than a pea nestled inside the transparent belly of a cut glass hen. He went over and picked it up, handling the small piece, shaking the chicken gently to hear the murmuring rattle inside.

"You don't look like no crank cooker," the boy said after a while.

"And what would you know about that? Boy your age shouldn't."

"I know plenty, I guess."

Gravel crunched outside and the long lance of a single headlight swathed the outside dark before the engine shuddered and the light went out.

"Go on to the back, Chief."

The boy obeyed. Packer returned to his place on the couch and waited.

Drema came in alone, carrying a small treasure of groceries in plastic bags. She did not drop them when she saw Packer in her living room.

"I'm surprised it took you this long, Pack," she said. She moved to the kitchen to put the bags on the counter. If she drew a knife from the butcher's block, he did not see it. "Where's Bobby?" she asked.

"Don't worry, I'm not here to do any little boys harm."

"Bobby, honey, you in here?" she called toward the back of the trailer, her voice betraying a high strain.

He had not expected her to be pretty still. Not with what he'd heard about the company she'd been keeping, the things she'd been doing. He felt a revolt somewhere deep behind his sternum, a cry of desire that could not get over its own shame, and this desire quickly became a greater force within him.

"You and me, we need to go for a ride together, Drema."

"I figured," she said. "But Bobby's got to eat something first. You just gonna have to wait a minute."

He sat watching her as she skinned plastic leaves from sliced cheese and mashed it between two slices of mayonnaise gunked bread. She carried it back to the boy on a paper plate and Packer could hear them talking softly. When she came back she was wearing a light rain coat that fell to her knees and hissed against her thighs as she walked past and straight out of the trailer into the humming night.

Once Packer had caught up with her, he led her down to where he had hidden the truck and opened the passenger door for her before circling around and getting in.

"You want a sip?" he said, holding out the bourbon.

"I could go for something a little stronger."

"That's part of the problem, isn't it?"

"I guess it is."

He cranked the truck and spun the wheel so that they jumped the hard ruts and met the asphalt, running a deep long rumble that tickled up from the metal floor along the backs of their legs and up their spines. The angles of the mountains floated beneath them like the easy swell of an ocean.

"I got a real need to care for that boy," Drema said. "He doesn't have anybody else in the world but me. Anybody that counts, anyway."

"What you need doesn't matter anymore."

"I'm sick, Pack. Don't you understand?"

He tightened his grip on the thin neck of the steering wheel. "Yeah, I understand."

He could hear something in her voice, something that was more human than it ought to be. He decided to put it out of his mind.

"Whose is he? The boy I mean."

She looked out into the rivering night.

"I think you can guess."

He swung them up the access ramp to the parkway, the quieted traffic of the main roads slinking behind as they climbed up the gentle sweep to the ridge. In a matter of a few silent minutes, the immediate peace of the emptied city became a dim shade painted in the low distance. Putting all of that back there made it easier somehow, made the way back to Cab more real, the past meeting the present in such a way that all the intervening regret and hate had become longitude lines running in fatal, relentless parallels.

"So you're caring for the child of the man that killed your own husband," Packer said.

"The boy can't help who his father was."

"Were you fucking him?"

Before she could answer he edged over to the overlook and braked as they came to the stone retaining wall, cutting the headlights and killing the engine. They sat listening to the hood ticking.

"You know I'm sick, Pack. It's like a disease or something."

"You said that."

He turned to her, putting his hands under her coat and blouse to feel her nipples as they rose beneath the pads of his fingers. His mouth opened against hers. For a while, each of them sought something in the other.

"Why is it like this?" she asked once he had pulled away.

Packer removed the keys from the ignition and pocketed them before he leaned over and unholstered the pistol, placing it on the dashboard within Drema's reach. She did not flinch when she saw it.

"Maybe the war made me different," he said.

"No. You were always different, Pack."

The pistol was between them now. There was no way to turn back from the fact of that. He wondered if he had placed it there to make the world swing around on a new axis, to inflict a change from the simple heartbreak of a normal day—the rhythm of what was meant to be forever interrupted and forever imperfect. That sheer grave weight cocooned somewhere in the chambers of the gun. Now there was no avoiding it.

"Did you kill a lot of people over there?"

For some reason the question surprised him. In truth, he did not know, though he must have. So much was seen through the green wash of the thermal scope aboard the Abrams tank, the slurry of enemy heat signatures blurring his memory into a kind of digital dream. The enemy hulks would present themselves and the tank commander would give the command to fire. Packer would ease the reticle in place and send the sabot rounds down range, the turret rocking from the cannon's recoil and suddenly the air becoming high and tight and acrid. After that, he remembered only the blind thrill and the desire to find another target.

He stared out at the looming night the other side of the windshield. He recalled something else more clearly than those moments in combat. It was in Fort Knox, when he'd first been trained on the gunner's station at tank school, sitting behind the hydraulic wheel that controlled the tank's turret. They were qualifying for their night firing, shooting at the plyboard silhouettes of Soviet produced fighting vehicles and the humped shapes that were supposed to represent entrenched infantry, the two dimensions of the war they were all being prepared to fight. The night erupted in tracers from the coaxial machine guns, the 7.62 millimeters opening up a small world of daylight all along the firing line, ripping up earth and targets impartially. And despite the hell of noise and steel, he saw the deer at the edge of the clearing, milky shapes in the thermal imaging, dancing into the lanes of fire. There had been at least twenty that strayed into the firing range. Immediately, excitement entered him, the prospect of live targets, followed by the urgent cry of the tank commander to shoot the fuckers down. And he had, all the tanks on the line had adjusted their fire towards the deer, strafing the animals with the three second bursts the tankers had been taught. When it was over, the satisfaction he felt was electric.

"Something happened to us a long time ago, Drema," he said, knowing she could have no more idea what he meant by that than he did. Still, he felt better speaking the words, convinced of their truth in the way a man waking can understand the rightness of things left behind in a poorly remembered dream.

"Do you think people change?" she asked in a whisper, her hand moving towards the pistol. He watched the bones of her wrist and arm under the paint of shadowed skin. When she gripped the gun firmly in her fist and placed the barrel between her lips she seemed to part from herself, dividing the seconds into true slowness through the simple act of physical will. He admired her strength—too well he realized. Too well to let her take the burden from him. He unwrapped her fingers from around the chamber one by one and held the pistol, welcoming the deadly weight of it as the sum total of whatever he believed was the correct end of right and wrong. Time did not stop, though he wished it might.

"I used to love you," he said, measuring the words for their truth before continuing. "But I can't kill for something I don't believe in any more. And I'm not letting you do it either."

She did not begin crying until he started the truck and pulled back towards the road to take her home. By then he did not understand the wetness on her face or the smallness of her suffering because he raged with a new conviction. A name was on his lips, and with it the knowledge that only the best should be granted the favor of dying forsaken.

The Sweet Sorrowful

Stoned, still good and stoned, Pendergast lost himself in the highest peak of things—celestial alignments and divinations, the verities of a fate beyond his ken. The stuff, in short, of Real Bitchslapping Truth. It came to him as he stared out at the languid trout fins, gently wavering beneath the surface of the trout farm. The idea, the dull and heavy haft of what was to come cast its dumb nets somewhere out there among the fishes. In that moment, he knew the future involved his Nissan pickup, a water hose and a blue Kmart tarp, slightly but manageably torn.

The farm was grainy with the speckled life swimming inside. Hectic razorwire scrawled above the ten foot high, chain-link fence. Pendergast sat in the cab of his truck considering, smoking dope and considering, while the digital dashboard clock showed a peaked 4:32 AM.

He pulled the keys from the ignition and pocketed them as he eased the door open, the smoke slithering along as he stepped into the night. Still cool out, the stars sparked like bright chips in the High Above. *Wintergreen*, he whispered to himself, not knowing what he meant by saying that, the word coming unbidden as a hiccup. Pendergast studied the cosmos and thought about himself and the cold galaxy twirling in the fabric of universal fate overhead. Thus consoled, he walked around to the back, dropped the tail gate and spread the tarp, cinching the crinkling plastic taut to the truck bed until it lined the surface, then closed the gate again. Once he was satisfied it would hold water for the duration of the trip, he slung the hose and boltcutters on his shoulder and went about the business of committing his crime of love for the children.

The sick children. The poor, poor sick kids. Lord, they could get to Pendergast, stab down into his conscience with their hollow eyes and rickety postures. Come tumbling in on his peace of mind in a stumbling stream of bodies—babbling, spring jointed bodies—like broken dolls poured out of a yard sale junk box.

He'd driven past the place for terminal children three times a week for nigh on a decade. Slowed down and held his breath, tires hissing as he gazed over the grass lawn so green it looked like it was lit by bulbs, a pretty pasture between good fortune and bad, him and them. He could never pass by that place with the brick building set so blandly back amid the empty landscaping without wanting to give some pain to himself, something to equal things out. He even liked to imagine knives driven hilt deep into his thighs and stomach, but in the end all he ever felt was an increase in lack.

The simple brick building held a small army of dying youth inside. Cancer, leukemia, hemophilia. Blood and bone going to early rot inside that plain building set far back on a green, green lawn. A single man-made mossy pond had been scooped up out of the perfect green, carved into the shape of a teardrop or cartoon speech bubble. That pond was supposed to give the sick kids something to dream about when they looked out their windows because something about standing water was supposed to coax them from the wreck of death and set their minds towards a mystic beauty which, like all mystic things, was just a peaceable lie. It rankled the shit out of Pendergast.

Each Wednesday morning the attendants jerked the sick kids out of their small Walt Disney wallpaper rooms where they sat quietly dying. For some reason, it was supposed to improve their hopeless health by going fishing. The pond, however, was as empty as the air. Pendergast suspected the sick kids figured this out at some point, but they had accepted the stupidity of their caretakers and continued to cast their lines over the brown water with grim good humor. Of course, the corks never bobbed. The nets never bowed. But that was going to change, by damn God.

He jawed the bolt cutters in a quick, fierce line, snapping the links in the fence, and he passed through to the concrete apron. The nozzle was a bit farther than he'd hoped, but he had plenty of hose and it didn't appear he would need to move the truck any closer. Once he'd coupled the nozzle snugly, he spun the valve and the hose tightened with a live gush. In a few seconds water began to plop out the other end onto the cement. He ran it back to the truck to let the tarp fill.

His legs were moving faster than he would have liked now. The ideas outpaced by reflex, and the word, the strange shape of vague sound suddenly rose in the chamber of his throat. *Wintergreen.* Still no tickle of memory in the saying. No, there was something more than that. A dark room and children laughing, and he among them. *What in the name of hell?*

The tarp slipped only a few silver threads of water from the edges. He stirred his arm in the filled truck bed as he brought back each bucket of trout, their slick fish bodies bumping against his forearm and fist as he stirred and stirred, bubbles rising to his shoulder like they meant to swallow him. His skin grew numb from cold.

Once the water was choked with fish and the fill line slopping at the brim, Pendergast made haste. He cranked the truck, hit the one-hitter, and got gone. Too quick, in fact, the water surging out the back, carrying a good dozen or more trout onto the asphalt. He saw their wild writhing in the rear view mirror, but there was no time for rescue. Too much lay ahead and these poor few would have to be casualties for the cause.

As he followed the road, the sharp edges of predawn darkness began to creep in on Pendergast. His eyes felt rimmed with thin glass, the world coming in a harsh rush as the road blurred. He must have smoked too much dope and now it had begun to bite. The demands of driving a straight line had done evil to him. His blood beat up through his throat, and the name *Wintergreen* came again, but this time there was something more than skipping syllables. He was a child among the children. The room unlit and murmurs and giggles. They wanted him to do the trick. The trick with sparks in his mouth when he bit into the candy. Many didn't believe it was true. He could feel their eyes on him in the dark. *Wintergreen,* Sue Topperson chanted.

Wintergreen. And he bit and they clapped when he could feel the tiny fluttering flash in his mouth. Then they believed him and Sue kissed him moistly but pulled away before the lights came back on.

He swerved across the green lawn, the grass truly lit with bulbs from the great floodlight above the Charity Hope Hospice sign that fronted the pond. The soft earth began to give and melt under the spinning tires. Pendergast swore and gunned it, mud slinging from the back like arterial spray. At that moment, when all seemed lost, the tires gained purchase and the truck shot forward, pitching towards the face of the moony waters. Too much. *Too much by God!*

The surface impact struck him hard, his head smashing the top edge of the steering wheel.

He must have blacked out a moment because when he came to utter falling wet darkness he couldn't believe how deep the pond was. How quickly the water poured in. And then there were the odd creaking sounds inside his chest that were sweet sorrowful measures of music he couldn't begin to understand.

But that mattered only for a second because he saw a shadow of something swimming just past his windshield. The swerve of life and movement within the flooded world. A momentary grace within the water. He had given them fish, he realized. As many as they could ever catch.

Patient Monsters

An inelegant way of coming to this, Holcombe decided. Glancing up through the mirage of himself reflected in the glass pane, he gazed out once more into a night shocked with Christmas snow. Headlights chewed their way up the opposite side of the foggy gap before the oncoming cars crested and came boring down into the dark valley. Sitting at the restaurant counter, he watched for when the right car would finally come on.

The single on-duty waitress came back from the brewing station with the coffee and filled his mug. By the way she lingered, he could tell she was becoming impatient with his lack of interest. She set the decanter on its hotplate and stretched luxuriantly, making a sound somewhere between a moan and a purr.

"Aren't you tired?" she asked, rolling her hip up against the cold griddle.

His answer was to lift his brimming coffee and return to his study of the mountain darkness.

"Hell of a way to spend Christmas, right? Working in a Huddle House."

"It's not Christmas yet," he replied. "Not for another four hours."

"Well, Christmas Eve, whatever. Same difference. I'm not opening any gifts, am I?"

He wasn't sure how he was supposed to answer, but wished she would go away. He checked his cell phone clock and laid it back on the counter. Already they were half an hour late. He had expected this. Always the need to cajole at the last minute. That was what Holly would say to him, that there were emotional complexities he couldn't understand between a mother and a daughter.

The last time Holly entered the mental hospital she had stayed with her mother an additional six months after she had been discharged. Caroline had always been talented at making others believe they could not get along without her, successful in convincing those around her that she was the gravitational law that bound them. This was never truer than with Holly. No greater cause of all this time ripped apart from his wife than what her mother had mechanically arranged, piece by piece.

The phone buzzed on the counter, startling him. He answered it quietly, not liking to speak this way in public.

"We're almost there," Holly said, her voice already strained. He could hear the sound of windshield wipers. "It's snowing hard."

"Yeah, I know. How much longer, you think?"

She pressed the phone to some place on her body while she spoke to Caroline.

"Not long. We have to be careful though."

"Okay. I'll be here."

The phone cut out and he paid the waitress five dollars before going out in the cold to wait. He enjoyed the falling weather, the swerve of what was coming down, and the way the wind silenced the wheezing of the high electrical wires that swung alongside the road's right-of-way. He could even see the watershed back at the gap, the cut stone face wearing its frozen beard. It had been a hard season, bringing these early storms with their ice and wind, wrecking trees throughout the county. It had supplied him with an ample wood supply. When his classes at the community college were cancelled for the weather and he had nothing else to occupy his time, he would go out with his Husqvarna chainsaw and cut stormtorn timber until his shoulders bunched and his hands ached. Then he would pile all he had cut under the eaves of his lonesome cabin to dry for easy splitting. Already, he had enough to see his wood stove through the harshest of winters, but he would rather be skinned running than complain of a needlessly high electric bill.

Caroline's Subaru hove into view, its one dimmed headlight proof that she hadn't bothered with the simple repair he pointed out last winter. As it came on, too fast for the conditions, he drew his last Winston and lit it quickly, knowing and relishing how much she disapproved of his smoking. The car swung in to the entrance, fishtailing briefly before halting a foot short of where he stood, its single high beam impaling him below the waist. He could see that they were arguing.

He pivoted and went out to the edge of the parking lot, leaving black prints in the fresh snow, the old anger already rising.

"It's okay, Mom. Really. I want to go with him. He's my husband for God's sake."

He could not hear Caroline's reply, but could imagine the response well enough. He turned and strode back, an impulse to put his fist through the driver's window turned aside only when Holly stepped out with her overnight bag and intercepted as much as embraced him.

"Hey, Baby," she said into his collar. His cigarette smoke tied itself around her hair.

"Let's get on before it gets too hard to make it to the cabin."

"Aren't you going to say that you missed me?" she asked.

"I didn't think I needed to say that."

He took her bag and led her towards his pick-up, glad to be giving Caroline nothing more than his back. He had Holly in the truck, the heater spilling hot air over their laps when Caroline appeared at her window, rapping hard on the glass so she could talk. Before he could ask her not to, Holly lowered the window.

"Holly, honey. Didn't you at least ask him?" Caroline said, her voice quavering and tears brightening the corners of her eyes.

"Mother, it's not necessary."

"Steven," Caroline spoke past her. "Please consider coming up to my house for tonight. For the holiday. Holly needs to be with people who love her during the holidays. With everything that's happened. Please."

Holcombe steadied his hands on the wheel, not trusting his voice or restraint.

"Mother, I've made my decision. I'm going with my husband before the weather gets too bad. I'll call you as soon as we're in."

He didn't wait for Caroline to back away before he put the little Nissan into reverse and rolled back across the parking lot and eased down towards the old highway, leaving the restaurant behind them in the moving lacework of snow.

They did not speak for a while as the pickup huffed up the grade. The mountains surrounding them hunched their shoulders under their winter coat. Holcombe remembered when he'd first brought Holly out this way to camp at the edge of the national forest, driving in the summertime then, the sprawling greenery. All of that gone now to frost.

As they crossed the Plum River, the water spoke over a beaver dam slide. The tires shuddered across the wooden bridge before Holcombe turned off the surface road and mounted the long gravel drive that led on to the cabin. He slowed when the gravel pinged up from the undercarriage, watching for road obstructions. So much had come down in the windstorms of the last few weeks, wrecking the side of the mountain. At night, he had lain alone and listened to the storms attacking the woods, feeling like a lost mariner suffering the buffets of a malicious ocean.

Once he'd parked and gotten Holly and her few things inside the house, he went to the gas stove and put on water for tea. Behind him, she rattled the cupboards, indulging the old routine upon coming home, seeking out the few ingredients known only to her, the concoctions only she could remember without fault. When she had been away, he had tried writing down the ratio of cinnamon and local honeys, folding them into the drink as prescribed, but the truth of what she would make of the tea could never come through without her hand in the making. Every sip he had tried on his own had sat heavy and bitter on the back of his tongue or else finished sweet and somehow imbalanced. When he now heard her stir whatever ingredients she did, a part of his chest simply caved.

"It's cold in here," she said, handing him the mug.

He went to the woodstove where the kindling had long since been laid and lit it. In less than a minute, the stove pipe ticked with new heat.

"That's better," she said, wrapping up in a shawl and claiming the antique rocker. He squatted by the wood pile and fed a couple of hickory logs then sipped his tea.

"I'm glad you're home, Holly," he said after a long while. The words were awkward for him. Her presence made him nervous. She did not say anything, but laid her hand gently across the nape of his neck a moment before she drew away.

"You've kept working, I see."

He followed her gaze to where his sculptures were gathered in the corner. They were several months old, already gathering dust. But to her, they were as sudden as a thrown light switch. He crossed the room and pulled out a couple of pieces so that she could see them better, the heavy iron bottoms scuffing across the raw floor.

His ironwork had been true solace whenever Holly was away. His welding skills put to use in the business sector would have been enough to get them into a decent sized house in a good neighborhood years ago. But Holcombe did not want that kind of life, refused it. He would only teach other men the trade at the community college, giving them the tools to go on and destroy their bodies and minds in the grim hours of torches set against industrial steel. He would not kill what he loved. In sculpting, he prized the beauty of something so completely released from strict form. How could he not admire the accident of iron, the tearing of brute mass into shape?

She came forward and put her hands on the sweeping arches, the wormy weld lines, gathering each piece by sliding her fingers across the intricate tricks of the surface.

"They're lovely, Steven. All of your things are always lovely."

He hugged his arms tightly across his chest and watched her. There was something terrible and exhilarating in her appreciation. The way she saw what he had wrought was unlike what others could see. How much of him and her could she understand in the iron monsters posing in their metal confidence?

She abruptly took her hand away and turned towards the stove, reaching her hand for its surface, as if she'd mistaken its dangerous heat for the artwork tacitly dedicated to her. Holcombe moved quickly, trying to grab her before it was too late, but by the time he held her wrist she had laid her palm on the flat top. When he pulled her back, a filet of hand skin peeled away and withered on the cooking surface of the stove.

"Jesus, Holly. Why?"

She did not cry out nor try to cover her wound, instead looking curiously on it, as if the pain radiating from there belonged.

He took her back to the small bathroom and placed her hand under a stream of cold water while he looked for something to salve the burn. The best to be had was a tube of topical ointment. He spread it carefully over her hand and wrapped it with a broad cloth bandage as she quietly watched.

She wandered back towards their bedroom and he could hear her dropping her jacket on the floor, shucking her boots with two disinterested thuds. A moment later, the slight sounds of zippers and then the soft mumbling of her dress as she loosed it and crawled into the bed.

When he had collected himself and gone in to see her, she was laying back with the covers drawn slightly above her hips. Her breasts were full and molten beneath the silvering lamp shade. Her fair hair spread across the pillow like something that had spilled out of her. She did not look at him as he slowly undressed and folded his clothes over the back of a wing chair. This had always been the strongest connection between them, this mute marriage of bodies, a communion of skin and whatever passed for commitment. Sometimes, that seemed to be enough.

She would not kiss him, but pulled hard at his waist, drawing him down between her, her fingers separating herself and spurring him within. He could feel her natural acceptance there, the body's mind knowing things by the rudiment of touch, tenderness there if nowhere else. Their movement was long, languid and patient, and Holcombe shut his eyes to the lamplight and what he could see of Holly, entering into a sleepy reverie where their love was something sketched in a kind of fine, ambling grace, drawn on by the dream of what he imagined the moment should be. She sensed him coming closer and tightened her thighs to him, holding his cock deep, collared there. When all of their immediate need was complete, he drew away, leaving a thin messenger line of semen between him and where she lay still and silent.

"Can you turn out the light, please?" she asked.

He leaned over and switched off the lamp. Even after several minutes, her breathing did not deepen into the pattern of true sleep, but he did not say anything to her, knowing she would pretend not to hear him. It was never harder with her than during the night when everything between them seemed as insubstantial as prayer. He turned his face to the window where he could see the snow, not falling now, but as still as stratum over a land as broad to his mind as an entire country.

"It's Christmas," he said aloud but softly, then by degrees gave himself to sleep.

The sound of running water woke him. He sat up in bed and listened closely, making sure sounds of the stirring in the tub were real before he got up and went in to her. Inside the bathroom, only candles burned. She seemed unsurprised to see him.

"Something's not right, Steven."

He sat on the closed toilet lid and ladled water into his palm and over her neck and shoulders, watching it bead in a slipping golden chain.

"Of course it is, it's fine. You're home," he said, though his words came without conviction.

"No, you're wrong."

He helped her up and wrapped a clean towel around her, leading her back to bed. She would not lie down, but sat in the wing chair and watched through the window.

"I need to call my mother, to have her come get me," she said, speaking to the winter outside. "She'll know what to do."

He did not say anything. For so long, he had wanted to force something on her, to break his wife's alliance to this quiet storm that had loosed itself in her, bonding her to imagined helplessness. He realized that Caroline was only a symptom. But knowing that could not keep him from his hate.

He brought Holly his cell phone and pressed it into her hand.

"Get the hell out, then," he said.

He did not wait to see how she might look at him, how his electric rage might affect her, because he was subject to his own cruel madness now. She may have called to him before he found his coat and cap, but he did not hear if she did, blustering out into the frozen wilderness and putting distance between what he could not trust in himself and what he was leaving behind in the cabin.

He could not say how long he may have walked before he stopped, brought up hard by a lack of breath and a sharp headwind. There was a kind of drunkenness in his tempers, a dislocation of restraint that overturned the predictable lapsing of time. He sometimes felt picked up from one place and abandoned suddenly in another. For so long, the emotion was profitable, especially in his sculpting work. The drive, the compulsion to push through. But what had been true to him in the accomplishment of an object of art was useless when it concerned living in a world with others.

He turned his face towards the sky, waiting for the slim mineral glinting of flurries to pass through the moonlight. His senses became tuned to the surrounding dimensions. Between eddies of the wind, he could hear the sober trill of a screech owl and the tentative answer of its mate. As he listened, the two birds became nearer and their calls fainter and more intimate until finally they were lost to his ears. He moved deeper into the woods.

His pace was deliberate now, and he found himself studying the intricate arrangement of tree branches. The storms had made surreal confusion of the torn limbs. The wind's story was written there in the puzzlework of snapped and snarled wood, the harsh declaration of what stand could be made against natural force. Long dry vines were caught within the broken tree tops, crowning serpents knitting them against collapse. He desired the avalanche to simply come down. He wanted the symmetry of the moment made real by the sheer grace of calamity.

Holcombe placed his hand to the trunk and began to tear at the encircling vine, the binding elements of the poised weight of all that timber, waiting for the weight to claim him, but the strength of the trees was too great. The damage done was not enough to capsize what was given figure there. He sank to the ground and watched the snow drift through the smoke of his slowed breathing, waiting for the coming of some kinder storm.

Winter by Heart

A low moon slummed among the briars, providing nightwalking light but not much else. In the dead end of the year, dark came so early. Dark and the desire to dig up the slimmest fringe of heat, coax it out of the surface of any cooling object: car windshields, polished granite, black paint. Luke Messer would press his bare palms to the warmth still living in any such surface and touch his lightly whiskered face, imagining combustion when it seeped through his skin down into his hustling blood.

Once he passed by the ticking hood of his black Lincoln Town Car, his hands already growing cold from where they had lain above the engine, he staggered up through the totterings of old family headstones, stepping over graven names that meant nothing to him. *Kin but not kind.* He'd read that somewhere, taken the lesson from among his father's forgotten books, but now it supplied nothing more than wasted breath.

Luke knew Old Carter Marsh camped the other side of these woods, hunched in one of these pocket ridges, making do year-round in little more than a dugout, stirring meal and wild meat over an open fire, untroubled by a world that allowed no place for him. Tonight Luke would find him, speak with him, have this damn thing done, and live with whatever sins might ensue.

He had come out this way for several nights before, always at this early evening hour and always alone, mending his fear with whiskey or cigarettes, drugging good reason into stupor. But even the benefit of a fogged mind could not turn back the fright when he beheld Marsh beneath the slung tin roof, still as Sanskrit. All resolve would seep away, abetted by the darkness between them, and he would go back the way he had come. But not this night.

No torture was worse than loving a woman you shouldn't. Luke knew that the moment his father brought Alice Forester home, that Sunday afternoon just a few months gone. She had stood in the doorway in the May heat, tall and picnic pink, speaking his Christian name as though there were some impressive weight in its saying; then she came forward and shook his hand.

She and his father married three weeks later. A ceremony under heavy June boughs, followed by a white tent reception with buckets of bottled beer. Luke, still only nineteen, secreted a few extra bottles and went off by himself under a tulip poplar to drink the sweating beer while he watched the others dance until the twilight lowered. All that evening he tried to pretend he did not think the warm thoughts he did as his father and Alice turned beneath the festive light, embracing one another under the summer balm.

In early autumn, his father began to travel, gone from the house sometimes a week or more at a time. Since leaving high school, Luke had gotten hired on in the early morning shift, preloading boxes into the backs of UPS trucks. He soon settled into the work, liking the predawn drive into the warehouse, sodium lights flickering over empty streets. When he quit for the day after four short but busy hours, the rest of the world was just waking up, and as he drove back across the stream of incoming workers, muscle tired and satisfied, he felt he'd discovered some secret knowledge of how a man could make himself happy with his own idea of what was right and necessary.

After sleeping through most of the day he would deer hunt up on Stoneman's Ridge in the late afternoons, walking the treeline where the shed acorns were likely to draw prey. Luke had never been a good hunter, too easily restless to stay put for more than a few minutes at a time, so the outings were really nothing more than long walks through the woods, stopping and listening, the rifle levered over his shoulder. Sometimes, he would flush an animal out...a rabbit scuttling through the underbrush or maybe a squirrel treeing and shouting down at him for his trespass.

Once he had been thus spied, he would find a good flat place to sit, a stone or downed trunk, and burn a smoke or disgorge a little whiskey from his flask before heading back down the hill to the house.

He had just been outed by a pair of crows who were cawing furiously when he decided his hunting for the day was very well done. Leaning against a big pine, he cradled the Marlin across his body with the barrel trained upwind in case anything happened upon him.

He pulled out his matches and Camels. A thrice struck match caught behind his shelter hand. He took one long, perfect draw, and then, as though it had been bestowed noiselessly from the earth, a black bear cub appeared no more than a dozen yards away.

The first hard stab of shock quickly gave itself over to nerves. Luke scanned the area, looking for signs of the protective mother, but he heard nothing, saw nothing. Nothing saw him back. The cub remained.

Luke spoke to the cub, laughing, yelling nonsense, idle threats. Then he barked and windmilled his arms, anything he could imagine to spook the bear, but that too only invited the cub's bemused attention. He squatted at the base of the tree, finished off the cigarette and warmed himself with a bubbling of the whiskey. Then he raised the Marlin and fired a shot through the cub's heart.

The cub went down immediately. Luke walked over and looked at him a moment before toeing him over to see the exit wound in the back. No wicked bone or pinkly torn flesh, just a larger darkening of blood upon exit than entry. He gathered the cub by its hind paws and headed back down towards the house.

By the time he came to the edge of the yard it was already full dark and all the house lights were on. He was halfway towards the old barn before he sensed Alice sitting outside on the porch smoking a cigarette in the gentle abrasions of the evening shadows. He stopped and they looked at one another for a full minute without speaking.

"That's a hell of a thing you've done," she eventually said.

There was no correction in her voice, he noted. He came forward and laid the corpse at the edge of the porch, just a few inches from her painted toenails. For a moment, he thought she might reach down and begin to pet it.

"What do you plan on doing with that?"

He shrugged his shoulders and leaned the rifle's barrel against the porch then placed his hands over the cub's lifeless eyes. Not knowing what caused him to do so, he quickly drew back. "I don't know. I want to keep it though."

She exhaled lung smoke. "I imagine you would. Take it on out there. I'll go get your Daddy's skinning knives."

He watched her go inside then hefted the cub and went out to the barn. The only lighting was a single yellow bulb hung from a long wire. He flipped the switch on and the barn's interior became an uneasy sea of swaying illumination as the gusting wind set the light bulb in motion. He laid the cub down on its side and witnessed the lengthening shadows stretch out and away as the bulb swung back. Not liking this, he moved the cub onto its back so it resembled nothing other than the dead thing it did.

When Alice came, she had the knives wrapped in a white hand towel. She set them aside then doubled the towel, drew her dress to her thighs and knelt on it. When Luke did not reach for the smaller knife, she took it up and slit the cub's crotch, detaching the wormy penis and slicing up until the pale belly was bared. Then, she repeated the meridian of the cut, this time slipping the blade into the muscle and fat until the innards began to swell up through the smiling incision.

Her hands worked quickly and Luke could hear the gentle suckling noise as the diaphragm separated from the bear's cavity and slopped onto the straw ground. She was blood dark from fingertips to wrists.

"You go on and bury that," she said, nodding at the pile of entrails without looking at him. "I'll take care of the hide."

He did as she instructed, catching the warm organs into his arms and holding them close as a baby as he walked around back and rested them among some creeping vine. He found one of the shovels back near the rear door that had been nailed shut and began digging by the slim cracks of light than shone from between the vertical slats. The earth was soft and black and he met few stones. He dug deeper than he needed to, not wanting to go back inside too soon. Even when the grave was ready, he smoked a cigarette and studied Ursa Minor above without knowing that the constellation had such a name nor understanding the portent if he had. When the smoke burned his fingers, he nudged the guts into the hole along with the butt, covered them and went back inside.

Alice greeted him with a smile, the black skin spread out as neatly as a pair of child's washed pajamas. The corpse was naked except for the head.

"You'll need to salt this down if you mean to keep it," she said. "I'll wrap everything else up for the freezer. Go fetch the handsaw."

He did so. She talked to him as she set the teeth of the saw across the small neck, decapitating the cub and quartering what remained.

"You wouldn't think by how I look I would know how to do this, would you? My daddy, he was a layabout, always up in the bed with books. Left my Mama and me to make do. He couldn't work, said he had these migraines. Said it was a curse of being a brilliant man. So when Mama couldn't make enough waiting tables in town, she'd send me out with a squirrel gun to fill up the soup pot. Here, grab that ham."

Luke pried the cub's quarter towards him. He felt the motion of the saw shiver up through his hand as Alice bore down.

She continued, "I learned quick you never waste any meat. I couldn't think of a worse sin. Not than to let yourself suffer because you've gone squeamish."

She rinsed the quarters by the outside spigot and carried them inside and wrapped them in plastic while Luke nailed the hide to the inside of the barn wall with the white skin facing out so that he could massage salt in to dry the pelt. By the time he had come into the house everything had been put away, and he could hear the soft needles of the shower behind the closed bathroom door at the end of the hall. He sat at the kitchen table and thumbed through one of his father's copies of *Field and Stream*. There was an article about the effects of climate change on the migration habits of Canadian elk and moose that showed many bright pictures of the animals fleeing increasingly populated and hostile territories. The photographer had taken great pains to make the creatures utterly beautiful amidst the larger backdrop of their tragedy.

The door at the back end of the hall cracked and Alice's turbaned head poked out from a billow of shower steam.

"You smell bad. I've left a little hot water for you."

He watched her step out, cased in a short pink towel, and cross the hallway before turning into her bedroom, the light catching the spangling traces of moisture along the backs of her long slim legs.

After showering, he went to his room and lay on the bed in his boxer shorts and a white tee shirt, holding one of the *Foxfire* books he always kept on the shelf but rarely opened. But while his eyes looked at the print and the pictures, his mind registered neither. He could think of nothing but Alice and how she had done what she had with the cub without question or complaint, and he thought too what it might be like if they stood together under the shower head, their compliant bodies meeting under the hot water and finally welding fast.

There was a tap at the door, rousing him. As he sat up, the heavy book slid from where it had been spread over his chest and thumped against the floor.

"Are you alright," Alice asked, opening the door. "I saw your light still on. Don't you have to work in the morning?"

Luke said that he did, his words coming slow from his recent waking. She stood in the doorway for a moment, regarding him. The hall light shed the false dimensions of Alice's hanging night gown so that Luke could clearly see the true shape of her underneath. The smoke from her cigarette coiled over her head like something being written in the air.

"Daddy doesn't want us smoking in the house," Luke said.

She laughed. "This little bit won't hurt anything. I promise. Here, I'll put it out if it bothers you. I don't want you to get me in trouble with your daddy."

She began to leave.

"No, that's fine. Here, wait a minute."

He swung his legs over the side of the bed and took his own pack of Camels from his night table drawer. Before he could find a matchbook, Alice leaned forward and struck her lighter for him, their hands incidentally touching. She took his palm in hers.

"You look like a man, but your hand is soft as a boy's."

Luke shrugged. "I know it. Never would take a callous, just blister and peel." He studied the intersecting lines on his palm. Slowly, he drew away.

"You should find some kind of work that you're better suited to, Luke. Loading boxes isn't fit for a monkey. I worry that you don't think well enough of yourself. Your daddy thinks the same thing."

Luke's eyes could not find her face.

"You and him talk about me?"

"We're concerned."

"I'm fine. I don't know why you'd care."

They sat together on the edge of the bed. A gentle lick from a night singing bobwhite interrupted the silence and then ceased, its voice seeming to shrink the world and make all souls within it suddenly beyond reach.

"I worry that you're lonely," Alice said. "I know what that feels like. Do you think all loneliness feels the same?"

Again, Luke shrugged his shoulders.

"Do you want to touch it and see?" she said, taking his hand once again, but with a difference this time, with a firm guidance that conveyed the dry warmth and assurance of her touch. "To see if my loneliness is like yours?"

A giddiness rose in Luke's chest, an awareness that was like a joke only he understood. When his fingertips grazed the soft pimpling of her aureole, he could not suppress a nervous laugh. She covered his mouth with hers then took his hand lower.

Luke could not remember her leaving when she eventually did, the two of them beside one another for a long fogged time, dragging shallow wrinkles in the top sheet of the still made bed while their hands made urgent movements against each other. Finally, sleep had taken him and before waking, the night had taken her.

With daylight the house seemed enormous. Luke moved cautiously over the pine floor, trying not to betray himself before he could see if Alice had gone out. Standing there and seeing and hearing nothing, he realized he'd slept through his morning shift work, but this didn't worry him. He went back to his bedroom and dressed.

Coffee had been made. He went into the kitchen and poured himself a cup and then went out to the sun polished porch, pulling on a stiff Carhartt jacket against the cold. Gelid light pulsed across the yard and mockingbirds cut aerials from the branches above, casting quick shadows on the ground. Alice's car was still in its place.

Luke liked the emptiness of the morning, the sense of time abandoned, and he drew himself into one of the corners of sunlight, leaning into it as though it was a patch over something broken in him.

A sound from the barn ended his reverie. The scrabbling of claws and a throaty growl. He set his coffee at the porch railing and immediately went out to it. The darkness of the barn took his eyes for a moment so that all he could make out were the antic shapes of low slung monsters circling one another and snapping their jaws. In a moment their forms became a brace of raccoons warring over the joints and pulp that remained of Alice. The blanched remnants of hands reached from straw muddied with blood. A few feet beyond lay the forgotten cub's head, left unburied from the night before. It had drawn some vengeful beast out of the night.

The wind could not reach Carter Marsh in his dwelling, carved as it was into the cutbank, the firelight scaling its walls, playing shadows there as ancient as brimstone. The dumplings and squirrel boiled softly in the blackened Army surplus mess tin. Luke watched him stir the potion with a long wooden spoon then rest it crosswise on the wobbly handle.

"I seen you come out this way before," Carter Marsh said finally. "I seen you studying on me."

He was not as old as Luke had suspected him from a distance. He seemed to still have most of his teeth, and by the corded muscles in his forearms, he could tell the old man retained physical strength.

"I don't think you believe you can run me off. Not if you've got good sense, anyhow," Marsh said, hocking phlegm. "This stretch of woods used to be my daddy's place. See that old chimney right there," he pointed out into a black night that could reveal no standing architecture. "That was the old homeplace before it burnt down in fifty-seven. I be damned if some pup thinks he can run me out of the holler where I was born just cause some goddamn chit of paper says something different."

"I'm not trying to run no one off," Luke answered. "I need you to do something for me. Something I got coming." He brought out the hatchet still in its Army green scabbard and slid it gently towards the hermit.

Marsh studied Luke deep, not moving save for the slight shuffling of his eyes, as if they were turning the pages of whatever truth lay behind the image before them.

"Son, I just believe you might be crazier than I am, and that's something sure enough that scares me."

His father invited what little he knew of Alice's family to the funeral, a sister up in Boone and a pair of semi-retired female cousins who ran an antiques and curio store over in Brevard, but they did not come the day she was lowered into the ground nor did they send their regrets. He told Luke that Alice had spoken rarely of her kin and when she had the telling had not been the kind of stories he would wish to repeat.

The attendees then, had been the same cousins and uncles that populated every gathering of bereavement Luke could remember from the time since his own mother had died from the sleeping heart murmur more than a decade before. Their condolences seemed well worn in their mouths, as if the words had been brought down from familiar closets and fitted into their silver jointed throats. Recordings of recordings, played out with the grim monotony of static.

After the benediction had been spoken and Alice lowered into the family ground beside Luke's mother, his father had opened the door for Luke to get in his truck and they had driven away from the shocked expressions of those relatives preparing to bake proper funeral meats and gather at the Messer household. Luke watched the dusty commotion receding in the rear view mirror but said nothing to his father, pleased to be driving away from Alice's death rather than towards the false remembrance of it. He did not speak to his father because his own voice could not be so easily harnessed as the words of those who did not know Alice had, knowing as he did the accumulation of true sorrow and the terrible ringing silence at the center of remorse.

They drove for hours, following the interstate down from the mountains and into the calm winter brown ocean of Tennessee. The radio crackled with occasional country music and, as they moved further west, the imperious voices of Baptists. Concrete islands of corporate truck stops stumbled past.

Luke's father exited onto a rural highway and they rode down the long pine corridor, passing the occasional hump of road kill. On each side orange survey tape girding the tree trunks marked trail heads for late season deer hunters, their farm trucks and half-crippled sedans parked hood to trunk along the narrow shoulder.

Amid the similarity, Luke's father turned down one of the clay drives and bounced the truck hard over the rain cut surface. Within minutes they came into a clearing with a simple brick ranch home with a spread of cut timber reaching out beyond to a short, bristling horizon. There were no cars to be seen.

"This look familiar to you at all?" his father asked.

Luke said that it did not.

His father got out of the truck and slammed the door, drawing a pack of cigarettes from his blazer pocket, offering one to Luke before he lit his own.

"Thought you'd quit," Luke said.

"Yeah, me too."

They went up to the house. His father leaned over an empty flower bed, picked up a silver key and turned it in the lock.

The air inside was stale, heavy. The few furnishings sat under a skin of dust. No pictures hung on the wall.

His father drew a vertical stripe across the clouded television screen. "Thought you might have remembered from some of the old family albums. House your mother grew up in. It became hers when her folks passed back when you were a baby. Then it became mine. A house I didn't want. One that doesn't mean the first thing to me."

He tossed Luke the key and went back towards the kitchen. Cabinets creaked and banged while he looked for something. It was cold in the room. Luke went to the fireplace and jimmied the flue open with a poker and began feeding sticks in. By the time it was ready for a match, his father had turned up a couple of containers of homemade wine sealed in vodka bottles. He drew a penknife around the wax crown and handed it to Luke then opened the other bottle for himself.

"Most worthless shit on the planet," his father said, drawing his sleeve across the raspberry stain on his lips. "But there's plenty of it back there. Don't be shy."

Luke drank the wine. The sweetness overwhelmed whatever else might have settled into it over the years. He opened his palm to look at the key his father had given him.

"That's yours to keep," his father said, reaching past him and striking the lighter to set off the kindling.

Dry as it was, the wood took within seconds and popped as the pitch exploded within. He laid heavier logs and soon the warmth was a real and living thing at their backs.

"Why you want me to have it?" Luke asked.

"Because it's your inheritance, not mine. Never was."

Luke looked round at the thin wainscoting, the dimensions of uninhabited space that pulsed from where they sat, wrinkling outward like some veil of polite despair.

"You don't want me to live with you anymore," he said, pocketing the key. "You blame me for everything, don't you?"

His father tipped back the wine, bubbling it down to the label.

"I'm not about to have this conversation."

"No, I didn't figure you would. What if I don't want to move here? What if I don't want any of this?"

His father shrugged, raising the bottle once more.

"It's what you've got to deal with now."

That evening Luke drank sips to his father's swallows and when the night had worked its wear on them both, his father went in to one of the bedrooms and crawled across the bed with one of the empty bottles still in his hand, disappearing into the blank sleep of drunkenness. When all his idle tossing had stopped, Luke went out to the truck for the things he would need.

As he drove back from Tennessee and came into Sanction County, daylight caught Luke just as he passed over the narrow wooden bridge above the Plum River. Once he had crossed, he pulled the truck over to the flat clay bank and got out to see what he could make of the water this morning. The sky was low and seemed that it might carry wet weather, potentially good for fishing. He had known this river all his life and his return to it after the long night warmed him. He edged down towards the river with one leg cocked back against the slope to keep from falling in. He put his hand in the water, knowing it must be cold. Even during the summer the water could chill, running off the bottom of a lake as it did. But this morning the pain to his hand was simple electrocution. He bit down hard on his bottom lip as he tried to keep his hand in the water. It would not numb, the pain instead learning increase until he could stand it no longer and drew back from the stream, folding his hand against his chest like something hopelessly wrecked.

He wondered at the pain his father endured when Luke had entered the bedroom and splashed the gasoline on his sleeping body. So great when he'd risen up in utter shock, the flames whirling around his head, coming from some source he couldn't explain, as if it were the manifested agony of something breathed out through his howls. And then the impossible whiplashed movements of his father's body as he tried to lurch free from the fire consuming him. So great and dangerous and pitiful that Luke had closed and locked the door on the suffering animal and gone out to the truck, leaving with the first tickling of flames beginning to take the rest of the house.

His father had been the wick for all the rest.

With the house in Sanction County as his own, Luke did not leave often. When he needed food or supplies, he would find something of his father's to sell. A rifle or antique that could be converted to ready cash at the pawn shop. He surrendered the possessions, giving them into the oblivion of his own routine survival. The spareness of this new world enticed him.

His evening walks took him often by Carter Marsh's hermitage. For so long the old man had been a myth, a gnome of local repute who was simply tolerated among the landholders of the area. Luke had seen him a few times in the woods through the years, but never spoken to him. Since coming back to Sanction County, though, his walks took him closer to Carter Marsh each evening. So he had been coming out, drawn to him. Someone who might understand this self-invented language of all things meeting their correct end.

"Why is it you want me to do this?" Carter Marsh asked, looking through Luke now, seeing through to the other side of the moment, time disfigured and all masks laid aside.

"My hands," Luke said. "My hands have become too heavy." As he spoke the words, he reached his hands out with palms turned up like skin moons on the flat stump. "They aren't mine. They don't belong to me anymore."

Carter Marsh, knowing that the boy may have been speaking the truth for the first time in his life, took up the hatchet and slung the canvas scabbard free. He brought the head down swiftly across one wrist and then the other, two clean strokes to separate the young fool from all things that were never his.

Jack's Gun

My best friend Dale has always been a dog man, always taken to any retriever or shepherd like they were two halves of the same heart. As kids, a stray was a personal challenge between us. No matter the amount of bacon I baited to my fingers, the animal sought him out in the end, taking to his heels like loyalty was simply a matter of good sense. The better part of him is mixed up with the finest things a man prizes in a dog, so telling his best qualities apart from theirs can be a little bit of useless.

He was having me up to his new spread, a little seven acre claim of valley land not far from the old Lincoln township. The holdings in that part of the county have gone mostly to seed, but they draw out the occasional amateur photographer to document a bit of lost Americana, snapping pictures of Cheerwine and Coca-Cola signs tacked to boarded up general stores and pharmacies. A pretty but run-down sort of spot.

It was late summer and he was intent on showing off his pastures. Also, there was a puppy he wanted me to see with him, a bluetick that one of his neighbors had offered for a good price. He told me that he was a fool for any little hound and that he needed a more discriminating opinion before he went ahead and laid money on the table. I imagined light beer and a few steaks on the grill were likely to be a large part of the bargain as well, a fair enough way to spend a Saturday.

Just before I left the house, he asked me to bring up something to shoot so we could pass the time while the meat marinated. I'd meant to grab my old Mauser and the Remington, but I was distracted and picked up the first cased guns that came to hand. I didn't realize until I'd made the entire trip and pulled up Dale's drive that I'd taken Jack's .22 by mistake.

I decided to leave it there in the back seat for the time being, and went around to the deck to knock on the glass door. I leaned in and cupped my hands so I could see inside to the kitchen. There was his girlfriend, Janet, leaning in to the refrigerator to pull out a couple of Coors and waving me in.

"It's open, sugar," she said.

I slid the door open and stepped across the laminate floors.

"You want a cold glass?" she asked, already pulling one from the freezer.

"I guess I'll allow it."

She poured out the full beer, set it on the counter and hugged me around the neck. Over her shoulder I could see she'd had her nude photographs hung where Dale installed the home bar. There were three, and they each showed her in black and white, slipping her young body in and out of shadows like they were pools of warm water. She saw that I'd noticed.

"You don't think they're tacky, do you? It was some stuff Arlen took of me before I quit him."

Arlen was Janet's old boyfriend, a guy that spent most of his days laid up with a half pill bottle of Xanax while she would pay for rent and groceries as an exotic dancer out at Pleasers, just off Highway 19. Arlen had been one of those tortured, artistic types that would take the back of his hand to her to prove how much he cared. Dale put a stop to that with a Ruger and a few correct words. Janet had not seemed to mind, and for the past couple of years they had been tight as twins.

"No, I think they're real pretty. Tasteful."

She smiled at me like she was grateful for my saying that, even if she believed I might have been lying, which I wasn't.

"Here, take this on back," she said, popping a second beer can. "He's back there in the bedroom doing a little painting."

I found him at the end of the hallway, all smocked up and edging out the corners of the room with light brown paint. On one wall, maybe half a foot below the crown molding was gold lettering in curlicue script that read: TRUE LOVE IS ETERNAL.

"Shit, didn't know you'd gotten all Hallmark on me, Dale."

He whirled around and whopped, "There he is! Hand me one of them cold beers."

He flung his paintbrush down in the tray, slinging paint flecks, and stepped across the plastic covered floor. He must have emptied half on the first long guzzle from the can. He turned back and looked up at the script with me.

"Can you believe that cheesy crap? Lord. You should have seen the couple that sold it to me. All soulmate this and dearie that. Made me want to puke. Let's give you the full tour."

He showed me around, running his hands over where he'd made small improvements to the place since moving in. We finished our beers in the kitchen, tossed a few more into a cooler and went out towards where his horse barn and fishing pond were. By then, Janet was up in the loft in a black bikini, sunning herself and drinking a glass of red wine.

"Hon," Janet called down. "The Three Billys have been tearing up the compost again. I can see from up here where they've strewn it."

"Sonofabitch! Come on, Bud. Let's see to these little assholes."

Before I had time to ask who The Three Billys might be, we were down past the next gate and climbing a small open slope covered with tall fescue. The wind made a pretty pattern in all that swinging grass, and as we stepped out across the easy sweep, I could see why Dale might be proud to have a good woman in a place like this and count himself one lucky bastard.

We crested the top and met The Three Billys, each of them gazing blankly at us while they chewed mouthfuls of garbage and weeds. One shook his head and blatted.

"Goats, huh?"

"Son, those aren't just goats. They're atmospheric goats."

He went on, shooing them and grabbed a shovel from the compost heap. I sipped my beer while he scooped all the mess back into the pile. By the time he was done, so was I. He didn't seem to care that I hadn't pitched in.

"How's this business with Kathleen treating you," he said, relieving me of the spare beer I'd carried out and leading me over to a shade tree where we could draw up and watch over the fields.

I knew he'd wait until we were off by ourselves before he brought it up. He knew the whole dumb story of how I'd chased that woman all over the country for the better part of a decade, leaving my kid without a father for a couple of years while Kath and I lived up in Portland, trying to mend together whatever it was that seemed permanently broken between us. My ex-wife didn't help things with what she told my boy, but I deserve a little bit of what she had to say considering I took off with another woman.

"She's moving out next week," I said.

"Again? She does that pretty regularly, don't she?"

"Yeah, I guess she does."

The goats came back, circling the compost.

"You see Evan lately? Take him fishing or something?"

The last time Dale had seen my son, Evan couldn't have been more than eight. He had turned thirteen a couple of months back.

"Talked to him on the phone a bit," I lied. The boy still didn't see fit to come to the phone when I dialed the number and his mama answered. "I'm thinking of trying to get him to hike the Appalachian Trail with me sometime this summer. We'll see."

After we laid out there for a while and the goats seemed to lose interest in the compost pile, we headed back up towards the barn where Janet had fallen asleep. Dale wrote her a note that we were driving over to check on the puppy and stuck the post-it on the back door of the house—in case she woke up while we were gone and wondered what had become of us.

We took Dale's Dodge down the rural highway. It was a big old silver beast from sometime back in the late seventies, and riding in it reminded me of jacklighting deer as a kid. All that roar and rumble beneath the chassis spelled plain menace, and it made me happy to think how many hours I'd logged in the back of a similar truck, manning the spotlight while one of my older cousins would send rounds down range to put some illegal meat in the deep freezer. I remembered too those hours with my father and uncles on those trips, the easy time we had with one another, the way everyone was ready to turn loose of any gripes or grudges when it came to getting out in the woods together. To a large degree, that's the kind of feeling the word "family" is supposed to make a man feel, if he's true to what he honestly desires.

Years ago, Dale was married to a woman named Beth Anne Sharples. She and Dale had dated off and on since their junior year of high school, then lost touch when she went to college for her nursing degree down in Greensboro. Dale is a good looking man and lacks no small measure of charm, so he ran a little bit of wild for those few years she was away, tasting what there was to taste in Sanction County. As soon as she turned up working at the hospital, though, all that changed. Beth Anne had been pretty enough when she'd left home, but had a red complexion and always seemed to carry a bit of baby fat that made her seem older than she really was. When she came home you could see she had been active during her college days, strong but slim through the chest, shoulders and arms, muscle sculpted to her like a swimmer or mountain climber. Her hair had been cut short and dyed bright auburn. There was no way you could look at her and not see that the time away had turned her into a knockout.

Six months later Dale asked her to marry him and she accepted. I wouldn't know for several months what had caused him to make a move so soon. He was not recklessly in love, but it seemed to please his family that he showed intentions of settling down with Beth Anne, so I didn't give him hell for it. I figured it was his life, and who was I to say word one?

We got piss drunk together at his bachelor's party held out at his father's old timber camp up around Tickle Cut. This was when he told me about Beth Anne's tumor. Everyone else had passed out in the old converted barracks, their snores coming loud and deep. A fifth of Wild Turkey passed between us while we sat there, staring out at the moonlit slash.

"She's known about it for a while," he told me. "In the brain. Inoperable."

The final word was like a cloud of iron in the air. I felt I should have been good and true enough to find something to say, but while I may have written it off to the alcohol, I knew then that I was unable to meet him where he was, to comprehend the weight of what he had to be confronting. I simply let him talk.

He explained that he had to take care of her, to see her through whatever remained of her young life. I could see that he cared for but didn't love the girl. That thing that has always made Dale such a good man, his loyalty, had turned on him, made him subject to his own commitment. And he just wanted to sit and drink with someone who would listen to what he was willing to sacrifice. I'm glad I was good enough for that, at least.

After he was married, I saw less of Dale, but through other friends I heard he was not doing well. He rarely made plans anymore, and when he did sign on for a weekend of bass fishing or popping clay pigeons at the skeet range, something always seemed to crop up at the last minute that kept him from going. I suppose I was avoiding him in a way, too. I had chances to drop in and see if he needed help with what he was dealing with, but it was always easy to find reasons of my own to stay away.

Then it got worse. Beth Anne got pregnant. They could not have wanted to bring a child into that, but the reality had to be faced. Dale called me late at night. It was the first I'd heard from him in close to six months. As he spoke into the telephone, I could hear the rattle of ice cubes in a glass, and by his voice I knew he had been very deliberately getting drunk.

"The bitch wants to kill it," he said.

I just listened.

"She says it's not fair to the baby to grow up without a mother. Can you believe that shit? She thinks she's being merciful. Merciful enough to plant a knife in a baby's fucking heart. It's not Christian."

He went on pretty much like that for the better part of an hour. I walked out to my own liquor cabinet and mixed a big gin and tonic to get through it on my end. Sometime in the dead middle of the night, he said goodbye and hung up.

The next afternoon I drove out to where he and Beth Anne lived in a townhouse overlooking the back end of the national forest. She answered the door, and I could see she had been crying. She called back to Dale to let him know I was there to see him and said she had to run some errands in town. She kissed me on the cheek and grabbed her car keys off the coffee table. The front door slammed shut behind her.

He was sitting on the back deck smoking a cigarette and from the way his eyes looked I guessed he hadn't managed any sleep. I sat down and didn't say anything for a long time.

"She's moving back in with her momma," he said finally. "Wants me to clear out tomorrow so she can bring a moving van over."

I got him to agree to let me feed him, so I could take his mind off Beth Anne. I put some coals on the grill and lit the fire and turned up some frozen Bubba Burger patties from the kitchen. They were stuck fast together with small squares of paper and I had to run them under warm water to get the meat to separate. On the grill they popped as the fat met the fire. After they were brown, I fed them to him like medicine. He seemed to be coming back to himself.

Kathleen and I were together at the time, so I placed a call to her to say I would be staying over to make sure Dale was alright. She had me send her love to him and then we hung up on each other.

In the months after Dale and Beth Anne split, a change occurred that none of us could have predicted. It was a little as if Dale was coming back to life, coming back to the kind of man he used to be. He didn't carry the weight of such responsibility, the certainty that his life was going to be a long chain of suffering. During that time, he didn't keep in touch with Beth Anne. I'm not sure if that was his or her decision, but it seemed to do him some good to have distance from her, something to allow him to sleep through the night.

One weekend we had just come back from a fishing trip down at the dam spillway that had netted a few small mouth bass and more of a rock-hard hangover, but we were both in pretty good spirits considering. When we pulled up to his place, Beth Anne stood by the front door with a suitcase and a belly full and heavy as harvest. For a minute we both sat there in the truck, not believing what we saw. Then Dale eased out and talked to her. I didn't need to have him tell me that I should move on. I put the vehicle in reverse and got out of there without saying goodbye.

When the baby was born a month later I was made his godfather. Jack Tyler Barrymore. Born August 17, 1990. Died December 12, 2001. The same day as his mother. The same day as Jeffrey Hope, a man I wouldn't even lay eyes on for another ten years.

Dale swung us up the farm's long drive and parked under a big poplar tree. It was getting on to that time of the day when the sun was a hammerstroke on top of the head, and I was glad to wait in the shade while he went around to the side of the main house to get the old man to come down and show us the puppies. I could hear the hounds making noise somewhere down there in what looked to be an old pecan grove, but I couldn't see the pen or what kind of livestock might have been about the place.

When they came back around, Dale and the old man were laughing. I shook the old man's hand and introduced myself. He said his name was Turtlewalker.

"Bit of Cherokee in me, though you wouldn't know to look," he explained.

He told us that the pens were a ways back so we might as well take the truck on out there. Dale got the engine turned and growling and I got in the cab next. The old man spat, hiked his balls and climbed up into the Dodge. As we rode back, he recounted how the farm had been in his wife's family for nearly a hundred and thirty years. His inheritance of it had come through her when her father died with the understanding that Turtlewalker build a brick ranch house with his own hands, some contribution to the land and to the old man's only daughter in order to overcome the fact of him being a "dumb Indian." He'd swallowed his pride and fury for the sake of love. His wife was worth a lifetime of building houses, he said, and by the look in his eye I think he may well have meant it.

"This dog raising. This was always her idea," he said, turning his head out towards the shaded groves. "She took such pleasure in petting on those little things. Never understood it myself, but I decided a long time ago never to look too deep into something that makes somebody else happy."

"When did she pass?" I said, surprised that I would have asked a complete stranger a question like that.

"Bout three weeks ago. Stroke. Sudden as a hailstorm."

He leaned from the truck and spat. I just then realized he was chewing tobacco. We rode on quietly, none of us knowing what to say. I hated that I'd opened the door on something like that, but now there was nothing to be done, so we let it go.

The pens were back beyond a little rise. As soon as we got out, the puppies pedaled against the fence line and bayed in their small voices. Turtlewalker went around and opened the gate to freshen their water trough and check their feed bowls. Dale and I squatted there and watched them.

"Damn, I'm likely to take all dozen if I'm not careful," he said.

"They'll make good coon dogs, for sure."

Turtlewalker brought one out, a strong bodied little dog with the eyes of an old man. When Dale took it in his hands, the puppy's whole hind end wagged.

"Hell," Dale said, almost under his breath. "How can a man say no to something that looks and acts like that?"

Dale bought Jack his first dog for his eighth birthday. It was a German shepherd mix he'd rescued from the county pound. Named him Hawk. He was as good and strong as his name, and he stayed at that boy's side like he was glued to him. There's a picture of Hawk sitting next to Jack where they're both leaning over a birthday cake, each of them wearing a paper cone hat. What isn't shown is that a second later Hawk stuck his long snout into the center of the frosting and attacked every bit of yellow cake he could get. Instead of crying, Jack clapped his hands and directly followed suit.

The ease of that day did not fully explain what had happened in the few years since Jack was born. The miracle that had long been given up somehow happened.

Beth Anne's tumor had disappeared, simply vanished inside her body so that the promise of a full life stretched out in front of her like something too dear to be wished for. She and Jack were gifted to one another, and Dale was the witness of everything he thought a man should be happy to possess.

But with the certainty of becoming a widower now gone, Dale found himself at a loss. All his preparation for hardship was laid aside, and he tried to find a way to become a normal man with a typical family. It seemed so impossible to him that life had worked out. Having survived the worst, and with no real scars to show, he drifted into a role he didn't quite understand, turning in on himself and fading gradually away from his wife and son.

After that, we spent many long nights together getting disastrously drunk. At times, Dale would fall to a bit of idle woman chasing that usually ended innocently enough, but each night seemed to take him further down into some place that spelled complete misery. He did not confide much in me. If there was any mention of Beth Anne or Jack, he always seemed to find a way to make a beer or smokes run. I don't know why I let him get away with that for so long.

Not surprisingly, Beth Anne began to feel isolated, unwanted. She must have known Dale for what he was, and sitting at home waiting for him to turn up couldn't have been easy. Like him, she began to seek attention elsewhere. She was still a beautiful woman, so it was never hard. Still, her affairs remained discreet, by and large. But once need and desire gets tangled up, people are bound to wreck one another.

Jeffrey Hope was a middle-aged ER doctor at the hospital. He was a handsome, high strung man with soap opera hair and a fitness center build. He was polite and popular with the hospital staff, and though he was known to drink heavily off shift, he had the reputation as a reliable professional, the sort of man that inspired confidence in his ability to save people from the calamity of mangled automobiles and sudden eruptions of the appendix.

Beth Anne and Hope smoked cigarettes behind the oncology wing after their shifts and slowly got to know one another. There was a little bar that had once been a true shitkicking establishment, but which had revamped itself into a rustic tavern to meet the expectations of yuppie tourists. After several weeks of this mild flirtation, he invited her there for a few beers and she had gone with him and later that evening ended up having sex in the parking lot in the back of his Audi.

They continued to see each other for a couple of months, often ending up in his home up on one of the big ridges that overlooked the entire valley floor. It's not hard to imagine the kind of awkward conversations they must have had. Substituting another person's body for some greater lack is never the satisfaction a person hopes for. Soon enough, Beth Anne broke things off. But Jeffrey Hope was not willing to listen. He began to turn up in her driveway in the evening hours, sitting in his car with the engine running and the headlights switched off. She told him more than once that he had to leave, that she didn't want Dale finding out about them. But the more she demanded, the greater he persisted, saying that he loved her in a way her husband couldn't, that he was willing to die in order to prove it to her.

Eventually, the situation began to frighten Beth Anne. She told Dale everything because she was afraid of what Hope might be capable of and she knew despite everything, Dale was dedicated to protecting her and their boy.

Dale came and told me everything. He was not in a rage, simply resigned to the fact of what he had to deal with. I guess the years of distance had changed how he thought of his life with Beth Anne. I guess that I understood something of that on my own.

He and I drove up to Hope's house and came up the long flagstone walk, shoulder to shoulder. On the drive, I had convinced him to leave his pistol in the car, though as I stepped forward and rang the doorbell, I began to second guess my decision to roll up on this man unarmed.

Hope seemed unsurprised by our visit, inviting us into his living room decorated with old family silver and faded portraits of men in military uniforms. Something about it reminded me of a museum or the home of someone very old. The large windows, though, gave as fine a view of the Smokeys that I've ever seen, and it was something else to behold that much country stretched out in one terrific stride. He asked if we wanted anything to drink, and in a few moments we were all sitting together drinking passable scotch. It was all stupidly civil.

"You know why we've had to come here," Dale said.

Hope buried himself in his lowball glass for a while, then nodded.

"I have no problem killing you, you know that, Jeffrey Hope? I have every right."

"I understand that," Hope said. His face was red from the drinking, but other than that he seemed unaffected, removed. I had no desire to be witness to this.

There were a few more words exchanged, but I didn't hear any of it. I was too absorbed by my own sense of discomfort, and when Dale stood, I was eager to be out of that place, away from a part of my friend's life that I should have never entered.

Janet made a plain fuss over the puppy as soon as we walked through the door, and it was clear too that the love was requited. It yelped and threw itself down on the floor, nipping at her happy fingers. Dale went into the kitchen and rinsed some steaks and set them in a plastic tub of marinade while I got us all another beer. As soon as I cracked into mine, I realized I'd let myself get a little dizzy, and not just from too much sun.

It was about that time Dale brought up that it was getting to be time for some target practice, and when he mentioned it, I very nearly let the slick can slip from my grip.

"Shit, man. I couldn't hit the broadside of the barn right now," I said.

But Dale would have none of it. He had seen me more than once cut bullseyes from fifty yards out, after downing a half case of PBR. He pulled out one of the old aluminum pie plates punched through at the top and sent me out to the backyard to tie it in place.

He told me where the shooting spot was, down the slow roll of land beyond the horse barn. There would be a long piece of cord dangling from a lone standing locust tree. Struck by lighting and as dead as midnight dark. I had hoped it to be somewhere off in a tangle of briars or beyond the reckoning of any easy survey so that I could say I couldn't find it, but as I walked out there I could easily see where it stood, the lone tree forking itself out there between earth and air, a long swinging cord hanging down from the limb where I was supposed to attach the target. I knotted it through and watched the silver dial spin in the breeze, casting quick slices of the sun across the scorched grass.

I turned around to try to make it back to my truck in time, to get my rifle out and say I'd forgotten the other, but as soon as I rounded the corner, Dale had already come out and was leaning up against the front fender, waiting on me. When I opened the back door, he was there over my shoulder, looking at the leather cases, so I had no choice but to bring them both out. He took one. I took the other, and by its light weight, I knew I had picked Jack's.

Though he was clever in how he tried to conceal it, Jeffrey Hope refused to disappear. He followed Beth Anne for several months, watching her, making detailed lists about her daily comings and goings. None of us knew any of this at the time. These facts only saw the light of day after the investigation was launched, but by then it was all too late, of course, as such things typically are. Had we known, we would not have gone. I would not have encouraged Dale to come up to the cabin with me for the weekend to drink a little beer and catch a few catfish out of my uncle's pond. By damn God I wouldn't have.

As far as the detectives could tell by the scene of the crime, Hope broke into Dale and Beth Anne's home a little after lunch on Friday afternoon. Dale and I had left from my house shortly before noon, but had turned around to swap out a leaky Styrofoam cooler for a bigger plastic one. Dale had suggested we swing by his place and try to patch it up with some duct tape, but I had been stubborn as hell. It was still before Hope busted in there, too early to have made a difference. That's what Dale has told me all these years since, anyhow, and I've let myself believe him.

Hope had entered through the sliding glass door and shot Hawk through the throat to stop his barking. He must have stashed the carcass in one of the spare bedrooms while he waited for Beth Anne and Jack to come home, so they wouldn't suspect anything. He had plenty of time to reconsider his plan. He even warmed up some leftover lasagna in the microwave and ate it with a glass of chocolate milk.

As far as the forensics team could make out, he hid in the hall closet, stepped out as they walked past and shot Jack first, through the base of the skull. Beth Anne appeared to have turned around and tried to attack him, because her entry wound was just a little to the left of her nose, angling up into the brain. Bad powder burns. Afterwards, he dragged them both into the master bedroom and placed them up on the bed, mother spooning the boy. Then he lay down behind Beth Anne, gathered her to him like she was his true wife and put the last bullet through the roof of his own mouth.

Dale and I didn't know any of it until the whole weekend was over. We'd left our cell phones at home and the fishing shack was as disconnected from the grid and as primitive as you could please. The only company we had that weekend was when my cousin Charlie came up late Saturday afternoon, bringing up the Browning .22 lever action I'd paid him for. It was a nice starter gun, something slim and reliable, something a boy could learn on without being afraid of the recoil or the report. I had thought it would be a fine thing for a godson to get from his godfather.

I knelt over the case and zipped open the long sheath, the rifle laying inside like the gleaming center of something skinned. Dale didn't say anything, but I knew immediately he recognized the rifle for what it was. The action was smooth because I'd kept it well oiled down through the years. I loaded the bullets down the tube magazine then handed the Browning to him. He turned the gun over once, gauging something in it greater than heft, then jacked a round into the chamber. The first shot sent the pie plate on the spin, the sun winking back brightly as it caught the afternoon rays. Three more did the same.

As the light began to fail, we put up our guns and sat down to supper. Janet had grilled the steaks by the back deck, watching us, not wanting to interrupt. We ate outside on one of the long picnic tables and listened to the evening birdsong. When she cleared the plates and left us alone for a minute, he reached across the table and took my hand hard in his grasp.

"I'll never get over it," he said hoarsely. "But sometimes I'm glad for what happened. Glad that that life isn't mine anymore. I hated it. Hated being a husband. Hated being a father. That man killed what I hated. I shouldn't think that, but I do."

His eyes were red, but there weren't any tears in them. I nodded and pulled my hand away. There were some places with him I just couldn't go.

"I guess I'm a sonofabitch now, huh?" he asked, though he wasn't really talking to me anymore. "Well fuck it, I'm a sonofabitch then."

I told him I had to head home before it got too late. He nodded and went into the house to help Janet clean up what little was left to do in the kitchen. They stood together, washing dishes side by side, their hips brushing against one another. He put his hand around the nape of her neck and she leaned into him. I guess that was what happy was supposed to look like.

I loaded up the guns and turned my truck towards the highway. It was late in the day, but still not too late. There's something to this valley, something when the sun anchors behind the ridgelines, a kind of finality to what happens at the unseen edge of the world, what might be uncovered or maybe turned back with one more crest, one stop further down the road. I pulled off and thought about riding over to see Evan and his mother, if they would have me for a few hours. I wondered if maybe we might be able to sit down together and share a few peaceable words.